An angry red suffused James's cheeks

"You're obsessive about doing your own thing," he accused. "You've shut everything else out—and everybody!"

His words shocked Roz into a brief silence. That he could twist the facts and make himself out the injured party, and worse, believe what he said, was too much. She laughed bitterly.

"Who shut who out?" she snapped. "No, don't bother answering. I'm not hanging about here to listen to any more insults." And not staying around, she added to herself, to betray her feelings by letting all her pent-up hurt come gushing out.

Roz had never voiced her suspicions of his cheating, had never flung accusations at James. She'd hung on to her pride . . . and would continue to do so now!

Edwina Shore spent thirteen years working in Australia's publishing community, editing mainly academic work, with a few brief forays into general trade or "bestseller" publishing. Now, when she isn't immersed in her own writing, she tries to work in her other interests, which include travel to Great Britain, Europe and throughout Australia, learning Scottish Gaelic, sculpting and painting. She is single and lives in Victoria.

Books by Edwina Shore

HARLEQUIN ROMANCE
2753—A WILL TO LOVE
2798—THE LAST BARRIER

Don't miss any of our special offers. Write to us at the following address for information on our newest releases.

Harlequin Reader Service
901 Fuhrmann Blvd., P.O. Box 1397, Buffalo, NY 14240
Canadian address: P.O. Box 603,
Fort Erie, Ont. L2A 5X3

A Not-So-Perfect Marriage

Edwina Shore

Harlequin Books

TORONTO • NEW YORK • LONDON
AMSTERDAM • PARIS • SYDNEY • HAMBURG
STOCKHOLM • ATHENS • TOKYO • MILAN

Original hardcover edition published in 1988
by Mills & Boon Limited

ISBN 0-373-02946-2

Harlequin Romance first edition November 1988

CHAPTER ONE

IN A small, nondescript room off Immigration in Terminal Three, the pale grey man from the Foreign Office took a statement. 'A formality,' he told Roz with a pale smile that matched his suit, his hair and the incredibly long, pale fingers moving delicately over the page, noting down her words as she spoke them.

He had introduced himself as 'Jones, Foreign Office,' in a sort of confidential murmur that gave the impression he was letting her in on a secret. The other man in the room was dark and wore a dark pin-striped suit and just sat there at the side of the desk, looking too bored for words. He hadn't said a word, not even offered his name, so Roz had no idea who he was and didn't much care; she only hoped he was not from yet another department and waiting his turn to go through the same old ground with her again.

She had been through it how many times already? There had been the young man from the Embassy back in Zangyria, not nearly so calm and discreet as the pale Mr Jones; on the contrary, he had been very flustered, if not quite panicking, at the prospect of an international incident on his doorstep. Next, two Zangyrian officials. Roz had a vague notion one had been a police officer; the other she presumed to be someone military, but she was only going by the medal-bedecked uniform which had looked as if it had come straight from a costume-hire company. Then there had been another Embassy official in Cairo when she had changed planes. And now Mr Jones—not to mention his silent colleague.

It should have been easier each time around, but it wasn't; it was more and more draining just to put words together coherently. She mumbled, rambled, backtracked, and there were moments—quite possibly minutes—when her mind simply went blank.

Roz didn't think she could take much more. She was deathly tired, her eyes felt as if they had sand in them, and she couldn't remember when she'd last had a decent sleep, nor, for that matter, changed clothes or washed. The perspiration and dirt-stained fatigues stuck to her and she was embarrassingly aware that any movement sent out wafts of something not particularly nice. Her hair was glued to her scalp in dark greasy streaks, while the black tail hanging heavily down her back felt slicked down with oil.

The interview was coming to an end; exhausted as she was, Roz could recognise the wind-down. Mr Jones handed her the pages he had filled while she had been talking, and asked her to sign them. Roz signed.

'Thank you, Mrs Thornton, you've been very helpful. And now I know you want nothing more than to be reunited with your husband, so Mr Ellis will bring him in.'

The dark man rose moodily and went out while Mr Jones smiled benignly into Roz's blank face. 'Mr Thornton has been very anxious about you.'

Roz found her voice and it came out in an appalled squeak. 'James? Is here?' She scrambled agitatedly from her chair, for an inane moment thinking she could bolt out of the room.

'Yes, of course. Your husband has been waiting for hours. Ah ... here he is!' Mr Jones exclaimed with avuncular, and quite out of character, heartiness, rising to his feet as James came into the room. Roz stood frozen to the spot.

She had known when she'd walked out on him that she wouldn't be able to avoid James for ever, that sooner or later they would have to come face to face again. But not now, not like this, when she was in a state that bordered on shell-shock, when she looked like nothing on earth, her hard-fought-for image of the competent, independent career woman shot to pieces.

'I'll leave you for the moment.' Mr Jones effaced himself coyly out the door, presumably thinking she and James wanted privacy to hurl themselves into each other's arms. He could not have been more wrong.

'Hello, Rosalind,' James greeted with the sort of soothing gentleness one might use on a frightened child. Very few people called her by her full name, and no one could make it sound as liltingly lovely as James. When he chose.

Roz ran her tongue over her dry lips. 'What are you doing here?' she asked unsteadily.

James made a sudden move towards her, making an indeterminate gesture with his hands as he did so, and for one wild moment, Roz thought he was going to take her in his arms, then, for another vulnerable instant, was afraid she might just let him. She gave a quick shake of the head and took a jumpy step back, painfully banging into the corner of the desk.

Her reaction made James grimace, but he didn't come any closer. He stopped and studied her from where he was, very carefully, his eyes combing her face with an intensity that made it seem he was counting every pore, and numbly Roz studied him back, with all sorts of crazy, incongruous things racing through her mind: James had recently had a haircut, and the black curls were a fraction too short; there was a shadow darkening the hard angles of his jaw, and if he was going out later he would have to shave again; his tie was askew, looking as if it had been tugged at distractedly.

James looked tired too, Roz thought, noticing the grey smudges under the dark blue eyes, but anxious...? About her? 'What are you doing here?' she repeated the question, feeling slightly more in control of herself after the initial shock of having her husband walk into her life for the first time in almost a year.

'They called me.' James jerked a shoulder towards the door to indicate Mr Jones and his colleague. 'They assumed it was natural I should want to be here when my wife flew in.'

Of course! And if she hadn't been dead on her feet and incapable of rational thought, she might have figured that out for herself. She could call herself Roz Davies, or any other name she liked, but officially she was still Mrs James Thornton, and that was what her passport showed. So, when she went missing in Zangyria, James would obviously have been the first to be notified.

'Well, you should have set them straight and saved yourself the bother of being dragged in here.'

The snakiness in her voice brought a quick scowl to James's face. 'For heaven's sake, Rosalind, I was worried! Is that so very strange?' James burst out in exasperation, running a hand through the thick black hair—an edgy gesture Roz recognised from way back.

'You needn't have been. It was all a mistake, anyway,' she told him shortly.

'I know that—now. Come on, let's stop arguing and get you home. You look dead-beat and about to fall over.' James's eyes showed concern, and that was the last thing she wanted from him.

'Don't worry, I'll try not to embarrass you by collapsing in a heap,' Roz returned sarcastically, then added brusquely, 'I could do with a lift, though. Thanks.' The way she felt, she'd have probably accepted a lift with Jack the Ripper if it meant a comfortable ride in a car instead of battling it out on public transport, because she didn't have enough money on her for the long cab ride.

James handed her her camera from the desk, then picked up her overnight bag and the carrier bag full of her precious films, and they left the room without a word, walking into Mr Jones who was waiting for them outside the door.

Roz caught something about some waiting Press people in his murmured farewell and took that to mean a couple of stray journalists with time on their hands and nothing better to do than hang around Heathrow in the hope of a story, but when she and James emerged into the concourse she nearly took a fit at the barrage of microphones, cameras, TV cameras. She threw James a frantic look of amazed horror.

'Leave this to me,' James muttered grimly, and gripped her elbow. Roz gaped and blinked while lights flashed into her face and disembodied voices yelled incomprehensible questions at her.

'Mrs Thornton has no comment.' Roz's battered ears picked out James's terse voice above the din, repeating the statement half a dozen times before he managed to get them through the scrum. 'Bailey is downstairs with the car.' James pushed her on to the escalator and practically forced her to run down the steps, and Roz had the rather fantastic sense of being kidnapped as he hustled her through the car park, which was ironic because, when she'd thought she really was being abducted in Africa, it hadn't felt like that at all.

Some of the Press contingent had followed them downstairs and were pelting towards them as James almost manhandled her into the back seat of the company limousine and threw himself in beside her. 'Let's step on it, Bailey,' he snapped at the chauffeur—unnecessarily, for Bailey had had the engine running and took off as James was slamming his door shut.

Roz fell back into the seat in a daze. 'What is all this about? Why was that mob there?' she asked after a few moments when she'd caught enough breath to talk.

There was a newspaper on the seat between them. James picked it up and handed it to her, front page facing. Puzzled, Roz took it from him.

The headline was so preposterously outsized that for an instant her eyes registered nothing but a stark black blur; then the letters came together into words. 'BRITISH NEWSPAPER MAGNATE'S WIFE ABDUCTED BY GUERRILLAS IN AFRICA,' the headline shrieked, and under it, 'Photographer, Rosalind Davies, wife of newspaper proprietor James Thornton, was kidnapped while on assignment for the Famine Relief Agency in the war-torn, famine-stricken African republic of Zangyria...'

Roz couldn't go on. She turned to James, bewildered. 'But it isn't true! All they were after was the Range Rover, and I just happened to be in the back, reloading my camera. They nearly died when they realised they'd accidentally abducted me, and they drove me to a mission station that very night. The only reason the alarm went out was because it took the frazzled doctor in charge there three days to arrange transport for me to the airport. I wasn't kidnapped!' Roz insisted heatedly, as if James didn't believe her.

'You should have tried explaining that to the happy throng back there.' James gave a grim laugh. 'Facts make for a very dull story, Rosalind.'

Roz tossed the paper down in disgust, and slumped back into the seat. 'I thought they were going to eat me alive,' she said with a shudder.

'They probably would have,' James agreed, amused. 'I'll issue a statement on your behalf tomorrow and put an end to it. They've had enough headlines out of you over the last four days.'

'Thanks,' Roz muttered, ungraciously. It was galling to have to accept a favour from James, but she knew it would be the quickest way to get the reporters off her back. Gratitude mingled with resentment. She said snidely, 'I notice you've been promoted to "magnate" for the occasion. Congratulations.' James ignored the gibe and suddenly Roz started in her seat. 'Where are we going? We should have turned off there for my flat.'

'We're not going to your flat,' James informed her quietly, but with an unmistakable edge in his voice. 'It wouldn't be a very sensible thing to do right now, because they're likely to be waiting for you on your doorstep and you won't get a moment's peace, so I'm taking you home—to my house,' he amended hastily.

'Don't be absurd, James! There's no way I'm...' Roz cut off her heated protest as she caught Bailey's interested eye in the rear-view mirror. Bailey had been the company's chauffeur for years, and no doubt was a discreet man, but that was no reason to treat him to a full-scale domestic row. Roz kept a sullen silence for the rest of the trip, but the moment the chauffeur had decanted them at James's front door and driven off, Roz picked up where she had left off. 'I'm not staying here, James, no way, and if you'd told me what your little plan was when you'd offered me the lift I'd have never come with you.'

'No doubt you'd have preferred to stay and face that mob alone,' James taunted tartly.

'I'd have managed,' Roz snapped back. What was a horde of yelling journalists compared to being trapped with James for a night?

James took hold of her arm and led her firmly up the steps.

'You're to call me a cab immediately,' Roz demanded as he bundled her in through the front door and into the drawing-room, where he finally released her.

She had not set foot in the room—or the house—for nearly a year, and had sworn she never would again. Roz looked around the room in nervous curiosity and experienced a peculiar sensation that she'd just returned from a short trip to the local shops. It was eerie: nothing had changed in her absence; every item—furniture, rugs, drapes, paintings—were as she had left them. Only the welcoming warmth the beautiful room usually projected was missing. It had a cold, detached air about it. Unused.

An involuntary shiver shot through her at finding herself thrown on to home ground again. Roz brought her gaze back to James, who was watching her carefully from just inside the door, her overnight bag and camera over his shoulder, the carrier bag in his hand.

'Welcome home.' He smiled sardonically as their eyes met and locked.

'That's what you think! I'm going to ring for a cab.' Roz started towards him and stopped. 'Where's Mrs Curtis?' she asked, suddenly aware how still the house was and realising the housekeeper had not met them at the door.

'It's her half-day today. She'll be in later tonight,' James volunteered offhandedly.

Roz started to the door again. 'You can't force me to stay here, James. I want to go home.' If she had been nervous here with James while she thought the housekeeper was around, knowing they were alone brought on something verging on panic.

James dropped her bags to the floor and moved ahead of her to the door, and stood, not quite barring her way, but making it difficult for Roz to leave without brushing past him. 'I haven't kidnapped you, Rosalind, and I have no intention of forcing you to stay against your will,' he said, reasonably, 'but surely you realise yourself that you're in no state to cope with badgering reporters tonight. I'm simply trying to be helpful, that's all.'

Roz made a derogatory sound, disbelief and distrust combined. She had been through a gruelling time, but she wasn't so zonked out she couldn't remember that she was not in line for any favours from James. He had never forgiven her for walking out on him—before he'd got around to walking out on her—and, for all his show of reasonableness and concern, she did not trust him as far as she could throw him.

'I haven't any designs on you, if that's what is making you so nervous, and in spite of what you think of me I haven't yet reached the stage of forcing myself on women who are dropping on their feet from exhaustion. Besides, Mrs Curtis will be back later tonight, so you really will be quite safe.' The smile playing around his mouth mocked her.

'I'm not nervous.'

A dark brow shot up.

Roz flushed. 'I'm annoyed and I'm tired and dirty, and I don't want to hang around here trading insults with you. I want to go home. I need a bath and a decent sleep,' she told him crossly.

'Then why don't you go upstairs and take a bath while I rustle up something to eat? The main guestroom has its own bathroom, you remember, so you'll have all the privacy you want. I don't dare offer you our bedroom because you'd read all sorts of sinister motives into that, wouldn't you?' James gave a light laugh. 'Be sensible, Rosalind. You're here now, you might as well stay.'

It was very hard to argue against something so reasonable. Roz was aware that she was hesitating, and that was her undoing.

'You'll have to use my bathrobe, I'm afraid, but there's still masses of your own gear around, so you can consign that rather unlovely outfit you have on to the incinerator.' James was smoothly railroading her by deliberately taking it for granted that she was staying, and Roz was no longer sure what she was doing. A part of her was telling her to get out, that she would be safer sleeping on the footpath than under James's roof, even for one night; the other part of her mind felt too worn out to listen. She badly needed a bath and a bed—both at hand just up the stairs, while her flat, two miles across town, seemed as far away as Zangyria.

Sensing her capitulation—and his victory— James lifted up her overnight bag. 'Come on, Rosalind. You won't know yourself after a bath.'

Roz shrugged wearily—a tacit yes.

'Good girl,' James said approvingly, as to an obedient child, and Roz felt like one as she went docilely upstairs with him.

Leaving her in the guest room, James went off to get his robe. He came back with one of her nightgowns as well, left behind with so many other things in the rush to leave his house. 'Your clothes are still in the wardrobe. Do you want to go and get something out now?'

Roz shook her head quickly. 'Tomorrow will do.' After James had left for the office, she meant, and even then, going into his—their—bedroom would be an ordeal.

'Suit yourself. I'll leave you to it. Come down when you're ready.' James was being super-casual, and if he was pleased with himself for having manipulated his wife back under his roof again, he was taking a lot of care not to show it.

Roz had fantasised about a luxurious long bath for weeks but, now that she was in it, she was too scared to linger for fear she'd fall asleep. It wasn't drowning that worried her, but James finding her and having to fish her out. Roz washed her hair and, cutting short the intended wallow, wrapped herself in James's towelling robe, briskly towel-dried her hair into dampness and padded back into the bedroom, feeling almost light-headed without the weight of the grease and grime which had soaked into her hair during her four weeks in Africa. With water so precious, none of the Relief Unit had had the callousness to waste any on something so trivial as a head of hair, and while for the four men it had not much mattered, for Roz, her long, thick hair had been a real punishment.

The whole trip had been that. Not just the tail-end of it, with its almost vaudevillean 'ab-duction'; the preceding three weeks had been worse. Roz had been shattered half out of her mind by the devastation wrought by the famine, but the thing that haunted her the most was the mental picture of herself walking around taking photographs, when all she had wanted to do was run away and cry. Some photographer! Lyn Barrett, her former teacher, and now her friend and agent, would laugh and call her a baby if Roz ever let out how she had felt.

And why hadn't Lyn been at the airport to meet her? She had got Roz the job with the Relief Agency and would be frantic about the fate of the films and the success of the assignment, if not about Roz herself. Roz had no illusions where her friend's priorities lay, but it wouldn't have hurt Lyn to make an effort to get to the airport, instead of leaving it to James to turn up and shock the life out of her.

'Rosalind, are you ready?' James's voice came from the bottom of the staircase.

Roz put down her comb and went downstairs.

James flicked an eye over her. It was not in any way a sexual appraisal, but all at once Roz felt nervous again, and vulnerable in his robe, with only her nightgown underneath. She wished she had gone and searched out some of her own clothes, after all. She clutched the lapels of the robe tightly together at her throat, and then immediately felt stupid as she saw the flash of amusement in James's eyes.

'You look squeaky-clean,' he told her, lightly.

'I feel squeaky-clean,' Roz returned, trying for the same lightness of tone, without quite matching it. She followed him into the kitchen.

James had prepared scrambled eggs, and hovered beside the table like a mother hen with one chick as she ate them. A ludicrous situation, with its overtones of domesticity—James urging second helpings, making more toast, pouring tea; wearing down her defences? The show of domesticity did not take Roz in for a moment. She had seen James role-playing the caring husband early in their marriage. Then, she had fallen for the act, hook, line and sinker—until James got bored with it and came out in his true colours as a very definitely non-domestic animal. And leopards don't change their spots. There was no way James was going to fool her again, and she wondered why he bothered trying.

'Feeling better?' James asked solicitously when Roz had finished her second—or was it third?—cup of tea.

'In body, at least,' she conceded with a wan smile.

James looked back at her without returning a smile. 'It must have been rough,' he said with something that sounded vaguely like empathy, only James could not possibly have a clue what a mental battering she had gone through in the last month.

'Yes,' Roz answered with discouraging brevity. She picked up her plate, took it to the sink and remained standing there with her back to him.

'Do you want to talk about it?' James had come up beside her. He put a tentative hand on her shoulder.

Roz stiffened, but didn't pull away, because at that moment she was having a lot of difficulty controlling the sudden trembling in her lower lip. Damn, she thought, furious with herself for the display of weakness. It was James's unexpected kindness that was responsible; tired as she was, she could spar with him—that was second nature now and she could do it in her sleep—but her frayed nerves couldn't cope with genuine sympathy. It made her want to break down and have a good howl.

'Why don't you tell me about it, Rosalind?' James persisted gently.

Roz shook her head in a tiny, barely perceptible movement and mouthed 'no' at the darkness outside the large window. She did need to talk; all those painful, searing memories and reactions would have to be talked out with someone soon or she'd go mad trying to suppress them. But it was not likely to be James. She had a front to keep up where James was concerned, and he had made too many dents in it tonight already.

Roz made a jerky movement of the shoulder and, taking the hint, James lifted his hand away; the warmth of it stayed.

'Don't go bottling things up until you have to explode. It only makes everything so much worse. You should know that after everything that's happened.'

Roz could guess where this conversation was heading. She swung to him, her eyes sparking dangerously. 'Don't lecture me, James. I'm not in the mood for it. And, anyway, since when have you become such an expert on what's good for me?'

It was funny how people actually literally gritted their teeth. She could see James's clamped so tightly that his jawbone looked as if it was coming through.

'You're tired and should go to bed,' he said with a too-conspicuous attempt at soothing her, which only served to make her irritation flare.

'Yes, I am tired,' Roz agreed with icy self-control, 'but not so tired that I can't see you're treating me like a child—or the dimwit you married four years ago and would doubtless like to have back in your clutches, to teach her a lesson or two for daring to wake up to herself—to you, rather—and for having the temerity to walk out on you.'

James was breathing hard, his nostrils flaring. 'You're being unreasonable, Rosalind,' he began, patiently, through the gritted teeth. 'It's understandable under the circumstances...'

'Oh, for heaven's sake,' Roz's control snapped, 'cut out the understanding claptrap before I scream! Next thing, you'll be getting on to my PMT or something. Isn't that the latest resort of understanding husbands?' Roz flung at him heatedly, then made a mammoth effort to rein in her fury and started again. 'I'm not being unreasonable at all,' she pointed out with an excess of calmness. 'I'm trying to tell you that things have changed. *I've* changed. I may have had a rotten experience back there in Africa, but I'm a big girl now, I can handle it. You might have caught me at a weak moment and conned me into staying a night under your roof, but, if you think that means I'm ready to dissolve in a heap and cry on your shoulder and beg you to look after me, believe me, you've got another think coming.' Roz looked into James's stony face with a taunting smile. 'Face it, James, I'm not coming back. I like my life. I like having a career, and one little mishap isn't going to change that.'

James had taken her tirade without moving a muscle, but at the word 'career' his mouth curled into the familiar, practised twist. She had hit a raw nerve there, and was pleased.

'Ah, yes, your precious career!' he snapped.

'My damned-fool hobby, so called. Don't think I've forgotten your picturesque term. Well, that same damned-fool hobby as made me into a very busy and independent lady these days.' Her voice dripped smugness.

'And much too liberated ever to need a husband again.' James dripped sarcasm. 'Don't let me keep you up, Rosalind. You might want to hare off to the Antarctic tomorrow on your next job, and surely even you superwomen must need to snatch an hour or two of sleep in between all those daring assignments.'

The sarcasm couldn't veil the underlying hard, bitter anger. Roz's triumph flared that she could still hit where it hurt James the most—his ego—then fizzled out as James turned his back on her. Perhaps he did so in weary defeat, perhaps because he couldn't be bothered trying to be kind to her and getting his head snapped off every time he opened his mouth.

Roz opened *her* mouth to say she hadn't meant to sound so ungrateful, then shut it again and ran out of the room, caught up in a confusion of anger—at herself for flying off the handle like a shrew, and with James for...for being James, contrary as ever: reasonable and understanding one moment, patronising and sarcastic the next. He brought out facets of her character that Roz hated—the resentment, the malice, the need to hurt—and that she'd never known she had until James had come into her life and changed it. Changed *her*.

She had been eighteen then, straight out of school and helping out in her father's antiques shop in the village. Her mother had died a few months earlier and, although Roz had toyed with the idea of doing a secretarial course and taking a job in London, her mother's death had made her reluctant to leave her father alone at that time, and helping in the shop had suited her fine. And, if she was really honest, the thought of moving out and fending for herself had scared the daylights out of her.

When James had strolled into the shop one Saturday afternoon, Roz recognised him immediately. Everybody in the village knew the Thorntons—by sight, at any rate—and Roz had seen James quite often behind the wheel of his Porsche as he passed through on the weekends he came up from London to stay at the Thorntons' family home about a mile on the other side of the village. She had seen photographs of him in the odd magazine, too—the social pages usually—but nothing had prepared her for the devastating impact of the crinkling-eyed smile full of perfect teeth and wry helplessness as he explained that he was after a present for his mother's birthday which was the next day. And yes, he confessed ruefully, he had shamelessly left it until the last minute and now needed Roz's help desperately to select a present.

All patter and facile charm, of course, but, with her limited experience of men in general and total lack of contact with anyone of James's sophistication, Roz had fallen for it like the proverbial ton of bricks—and almost fallen over herself suggesting one thing after another until, in the end, James settled for a pair of beautiful, very ornate silver candlesticks, and told Roz, again with that devastating smile, that he could not have managed without her. He had made her day, and odds were, he knew it.

To her amazement, he had returned the next weekend to tell her that Cecily had loved the present. Roz had flushed and stammered something, she didn't know what, overcome with the knowledge that James Thornton had actually bothered to call in just to speak to her. The following Saturday he popped in on no other pretext than to say hello, and she was well and truly smitten, dying a hundred deaths all during the next week in case he didn't show up again.

James *did* show up, and invited her for a coffee after the shop closed. And that was how it all started—slowly and carefully stage-managed by James. Their relationship, and Roz herself, were nurtured along like exotic pot-plants. James never put any sexual pressure on her: their lovemaking, if it could be called that, was confined to kisses, holding hands, the mildest of petting. With her inhibitions being what they were, anything else would have sent her bolting. James had sensed that; it would have been hard not to, because she was as naïve and transparent as they came.

It was a preposterously old-fashioned and, in its way, romantic courtship that lasted a year. Looking back, James's patience and restraint had been nothing short of impressive. But why? Why take on a hopelessly naïve nineteen-year-old for a wife, when he must have had his pick of any number of sophisticated women? Even at the time, and madly in love as she had been, the question must have been at the back of her mind, because when James asked her to marry him, Roz had involuntarily blurted, 'Why me?' then blushed furiously at having come out with something so gauche.

James had laughed, a little taken aback, then gently stroked a finger down her hot, embarrassed cheek. 'Because I love you and I think you will make a wonderful wife and mother,' he told her, smiling, but his voice had never been more serious. 'I want a family, Rosalind—children...lots of them.' His voice lightened. 'Dogs...cats—the whole menagerie. What do you say to that?'

Roz had said she thought it sounded wonderful.

And it *had* been wonderful for a time, before it became painfully apparent that James had tired of playing at domestic bliss and returned to in-

terests that very definitely did not include her—
let alone children or cats and dogs. Granted, his
father had died recently and James had taken
over the chairmanship of the family's newspaper
company. However, as months passed and James
stayed distracted and edgy and away from home
more and more, Roz began to suspect other
women, but felt too humiliated and distressed to
challenge him about it. She had no proof, and
James would have denied it, anyway. Instead,
Roz had had to find her own interests. Her photography did start as a hobby, but soon meant a
lot to her—no longer simply filling in the void
left by James's absences, but a means of sal-
vaging her self-esteem. She clung to it as if her
life depended on it, in spite of James's growing
disapproval and complaints that it was taking up
too much of her time—ironic, when it was he
who had driven her to it in the first place...

Roz had forgotten all about Mrs Curtis, and was
startled awake by the housekeeper drawing back
the curtains. Roz blinked against the sudden shaft
of light streaming into the room as Mrs Curtis
turned to her. 'Good morning, Mrs Thornton.
I've brought you some tea. It's on the bedside
table beside you,' the housekeeper said expressionlessly. If she had any curious thoughts about
seeing Roz back in the house, she kept them to
herself.

They had never been particularly friendly,
possibly because they had started off on such a
dubious footing. At nineteen, Roz had been

scared stiff of the gaunt, humourless woman who ran James's house with such intimidating efficiency. Eventually, they evolved a relationship of sorts, outwardly very civil, but Roz always suspected that the older woman thought her a silly little rabbit and wondered why James had ever married her—she and Roz both!

'Thank you, Mrs Curtis,' Roz returned with careful cordiality. 'What time is it, please?'

'Going on eleven.'

'Grief!' Roz sprang into a sitting position. She had wanted to stay in the room until she was sure James had left the house, but not lie around for half the day. 'I overslept. I'm sorry,' she said, guiltily, and then was annoyed at the childish impulse to explain herself.

From the door, the housekeeper pressed her features into a smile that would have curdled milk. 'No doubt it's the exciting life catching up with you.' She closed the door silently behind her, leaving her disapproval lingering in the room like a heavy fog. Roz pulled a silly face at the closed door. The woman had honed her put-downs to a fine art long ago, and Roz had learnt to ignore them. It was unpleasantly surprising now how much they could still sting.

Roz gulped down the tea hurriedly and got up, then, feeling like an intruder, sneaked down the passage to James's bedroom. Ridiculously nervous that Mrs Curtis would surprise her and demand to know what she was doing, Roz ran to the wall of wardrobe and slid open what used to be her side of the wardrobe, then stared in astonishment at the array of clothes—her clothes, untouched from the day she left, the drawers still full of nightwear and underclothes; the shoe-rack holding half a dozen pairs of shoes.

Why had James kept them all? Hardly for their sentimental value. Did he really believe she was going to return to him? James was an obstinate and arrogant man, and she had wounded his ego by walking out on him; that was why he had refused her solicitor's first and, as yet, only approach for an early divorce—to pay her back. Fine, Roz had expected him to be bloody-minded about that and was prepared to wait him out. James must know that. Then why keep her clothes hanging there as if she was about to return at any moment?

Roz snatched up some underwear and grabbed a skirt and sweater at random. Being in the room unnerved her; she had known it would, with its violent memories of their last night together after she had told James she was leaving him.

Typically, he had refused to take her seriously. Then, when he finally realised she meant it, they had had a row to end all rows, which had culminated in James taking her in a blaze of savagery. Roz had fought him with the fury of a wildcat at first, then, to her later humiliation, had responded on a surge of raw passion she had never experienced before. It was the first time they had made love—if that was the word—for months. Three...four...Roz couldn't remember, but everything else about that torrid night was branded into her brain.

She had left the next day.

With the clothes and shoes under her arm, Roz fled back to the guest room.

CHAPTER TWO

'THERE have been some telephone calls for you, Mrs Thornton,' the housekeeper told her as Roz was saying a flustered goodbye. She was on edge and irrationally frantic to get out of the house. 'Reporters. Mr Thornton advised me to deal with them without bothering you, so I did.'

'Yes, yes. Thank you,' Roz mumbled distractedly.

'Mr Thornton also asked me to remind you that he would take care of the . . . unpleasantness from his office this morning.' The look on the woman's face indicated she thought James was wasting his time on Roz's 'unpleasantness'.

'Yes, yes. Thank you,' Roz repeated, grateful that James had not forgotten, and that, after her display of temper and unreasonableness last night, he was still prepared to get the reporters off her back—by ringing around the major newspapers, she supposed, and giving them a brief statement about the not very exciting facts of the so-called abduction.

She caught the bus to her flat in Fulham. She had the ground floor of a shabby two-storey terrace house in an as yet unfashionable area, and had it to herself, paying a king's ransom in rent for the luxury. Worth every penny, despite the fact that, when she'd moved in about eight months ago, it had meant eating into her meagre savings. At that time, her spasmodic assignments had not brought in enough income to cover the rent, and she had been determined not to take a penny from James, returning every cheque he'd sent her out of what must have been his misguided sense of responsibility for her, or, more likely, the assumption that she was incapable of keeping a roof over her own head.

Her flat was three houses down from the corner of the main street and, immediately she rounded the corner, Roz saw the man and young woman hanging around her gate; they had the look of having been there a long time. As she approached, they sprinted towards her like hounds, confirming her worst suspicions.

Roz shook her head at them. 'You've been wasting your time,' she said quite pleasantly; two reporters she could handle. 'It was all a mix-up, and your papers probably have the real, very dull story by now. My husband was going to...'

'Ah, yes, James Thornton,' the young woman broke in with practised ease. 'That's who we wanted to talk to you about, Mrs Thornton.' Roz's expression switched to a glare. Undaunted, the reporter pressed on. 'How long have you been separated, and why did...'

'Mind your own business!' Roz hissed at her, storming past the pair in disgust, and only just managing to slam the door on them. She should have realised the gutter press would latch on to that intriguing aspect of the story.

The telephone was ringing as she burst into the hall, and continued ringing all the time it took her to unlock her own flat and let herself in. Lyn, thought Roz, as she dived to snatch up the receiver, but when it turned out to be yet another reporter she slammed the phone down before he'd finished speaking. What on earth would it have been like last night if she had been here? Roz shuddered to think and when, a couple of seconds later, the ringing started again, she was so mad she was ready to tell whoever it was exactly what she thought of people who senselessly badgered other people in the name of news.

'Yes?' she barked into the phone, and then needed a very long moment for it to sink in that the man on the other end of the line was her own father, ringing from Scotland, where he had retired to about two years ago.

The call did nothing for her frame of mind. Tom Davies kept repeating how worried he had been, how worried James had been and how James had kept in touch with him constantly. And why hadn't Roz telephoned yesterday, instead of leaving it to James to tell him she was safe?

Roz was on the defensive—guilty, annoyed, and glad to end the call with vague promises of coming up to see him very soon. She always promised him that, but had only made the trip once, and even then she was sorry she had gone to all that trouble to be nagged to death. Her father had been appalled when she'd left James— women simply didn't do that sort of thing in his book; they stuck to their husbands through thick and thin. It had been a waste of breath trying to tell him times had changed and women had every right to live their own lives. Roz had given up and could only be grateful that he was hundreds of miles away and had to watch his pennies enough not to harangue her too often.

She picked up the phone before it could ring again, and quickly dialled Lyn Barrett's number, gazing around the room in faint distaste as she waited for her friend to answer. The stale mustiness pervading the small sitting-room was from the flat having been closed for a month, but how could it have become so depressingly dingy in such a short time? The bright colours of the travel posters alongside some of her own photographs only seemed to draw attention to the grimy state of the walls; the faded, aged carpet looked shabbier than ever, while the new cushions on the sofa only highlighted the worn-out pile of its cheap velour. Grimacing, Roz shut her mind's eye to the image of the beautiful house she had just come from—James's house. Comparisons were odious, and you had to cut your coat according to your cloth. A stitch in time…Oh, stop it! she snapped at herself as her mind went off on its nonsensical tangent.

As she was about to give up on Lyn and hang up, Lyn's voice finally shouted in her ear. 'Yes, hello?' Lyn had an irritating habit of assuming anyone on the other end of a telephone line was deaf.

Roz hastily pulled the receiver back an inch from her ear. 'Lyn, it's me, Roz. I'm back.'

'Roz! Where on earth have you been?' Lyn bellowed accusingly. 'I rang and rang last night after I spotted you on the news—you looked frightful, by the way——' she threw in as an aside '—and I've been trying to get hold of you all morning. I've been in the darkroom just now, which is why I didn't answer for so long, but I was going to try you again in a moment——'

'Well, here I am,' Roz interrupted the breathless rush of words. It was not exactly a welcome, so it was just as well that she hadn't been expecting one.

'And not before time. Listen, I can be with you in an hour to pick up the films, is that OK?'

'Yes,' answered Roz. Then, as her eyes drifted down to where she had dropped her overnight bag and camera case on the floor, she changed that to 'No!' in what was almost a screech.

'What?' Lyn shouted back in her ear.

'I've left them behind...the films...' Roz couldn't believe it. The films were still at James's because, in her haste to leave, she hadn't remembered that James had left them in the drawing-room and not brought them upstairs with her other things.

'You left the films in Africa? Roz, have you gone off your head?'' Lyn was incredulous.

'No, no, only at—where I stayed last night. It's all right, Lyn,' she assured Lyn with a hasty laugh. 'There's no need to worry. I can nip back and get them and be here when you come.'

*　　*　　*

Roz kept the cab waiting outside James's house while she rang at the door. It was still waiting, with its meter ticking over at an alarming rate, when, getting no answer, she charged around the block and through the back gardens to try to get in through the rear entrance, only to find the gate locked. On a belated inspiration Roz asked the cab driver to take her to the nearest public telephone which was only in the next street, and tried to call Mrs Curtis from there. Getting no answer again she had to assume the housekeeper had gone out to do some shopping or whatever, and in the end gave the driver the address of James's office where, horrified at the fare she had run up, Roz paid him off and dashed into the building.

It was a very long time since she had been to James's office. Early in their marriage she used to come in several times a week to pick him up for lunch, and often they would even meet up after James had finished for the day, and take in a show and supper. It seemed they couldn't see enough of each other, be together enough. Her world had revolved around James then, and she had assumed the reverse had applied. How naïve could you be? She should have realised there was a time limit on her novelty value, and it had expired about fifteen months into the marriage.

Roz bypassed the reception area on the ground floor and made straight for the lifts. James's office used to be on the third floor and Roz presumed it still was, only to discover when she got there that the layout of the whole floor had changed. Completely lost, she had to ask for directions and was eventually escorted down a floor and taken to the chairman's suite. From there she was passed on to a typist, who in turn took her into the secretary's office and presented her to Barbara Russell as if the woman was royalty.

Ms Russell looked to be about thirty-five—James's age—and groomed to her back teeth, with not a blonde hair out of place. The severe dark suit over the white blouse looked almost a copy of one of James's own.

'I'd like to see Mr Thornton, please,' Roz said shortly, because the woman's cool scrutiny annoyed her. The raised eyebrow was obviously meant to do duty as 'What do you want?'

'Do you have an appointment?' Barbara Russell asked infuriatingly, knowing perfectly well that Roz hadn't.

'No, but I'd like to see him now. If you don't mind,' Roz added tightly.

'I'm afraid that's not possible. Mr Thornton is in conference. I can make an appointment for you if you would care to tell me what it is you wish to see him about.' There was a lot of officious flicking through the diary. 'It will have to be next week...'

In conference, my eye, thought Roz, and no, she did not care to tell the supercilious woman anything. There were two doors leading off the room, both closed. Roz cast a speculative eye at each, then dismissed the idea of barging at one of them. Ten-to-one, the door she chose would turn out to be the coat-cupboard or something!

'Your name?' the secretary enquired without interest.

'Thornton. Mrs Thornton. And I must insist on seeing my husband immediately.' Roz played her ace and enjoyed it fleetingly.

Barbara Russell was taken aback. Even if she knew James had a wife at all, she would not have been expecting someone like Roz, who didn't look much like anybody's idea of a chairman's wife. She had flung on the first clothes to hand in James's bedroom—a cherry-red woollen skirt and an outsized Arran sweater—not exactly elegant. She had no make-up on and, even after twelve hours of sleep, her grey eyes looked lost in a sea of grey smudges, while the only thing that could be said for her hair, which was drawn back into a ponytail again, was that it was now clean.

Recovering her composure, the secretary indicated an armchair by the wall. 'If you would care to wait for a few moments...' her eyes strayed unconsciously to the left door.

Roz did not wait. She made straight for the door indicated by the woman's glance.

'You can't!' Barbara Russell yelped.

Roz could and did. She flung the door open.

There were four or five men sitting around the oval table at the far end of the large office. They all turned to the door, where Roz stood rooted to the spot.

'I'm sorry, Mr Thornton,' Barbara Russell said in a strangled whisper behind Roz's shoulder.

James rose from his seat unhurriedly. After the brief initial surprise, his face showed no expression. 'Excuse me, gentlemen,' he said calmly and came across the room. 'Thank you, Barbara,' he murmured politely. Taking Roz's elbow in a grip that made her flinch, he turned her around and propelled her back into the secretary's office, closing the door firmly behind them.

'James, I'm sorry. I didn't mean...I've left my films behind at the house, and Mrs Curtis is out. I need to borrow your key,' Roz rushed out her embarrassed explanation.

'I see.' James turned to his secretary. 'I'd like you to order my car to the front door, please, Barbara, and you to wait here, Rosalind. I'll be with you in a moment.' James gave his orders with punctilious politeness and returned to his office, leaving Roz standing where she was. It did not occur to her to disobey.

Barbara Russell had a pinched 'I told you so' smile on her face as she spoke into the telephone. Roz could have sunk through the floor.

'I'll be away for the next hour,' James told his secretary when he reappeared a few moments later.

The smug smile left Barbara's face. 'But what about...?' She jerked her head at the closed door.

'We were just about to break for lunch. I'll be back in time for the post-lunch session,' James said, and only then did it dawn on Roz that the car not been ordered just to take her away, but that James was apparently coming with her. She came back to life in a fluster. 'No, James, I only need the key. You don't have to...'

She was already being led out of the room, with James's fingers digging savagely into her upper arm. Roz threw a nervous look at the stony profile and didn't say another word until they were out of the building.

'This is ridiculous, James! You don't have to come with me. I promise I'll bring the key back immediately,' Roz protested as James marched her to the waiting car. Waving Bailey back into his seat, he handed her into the car with restrained anger and, for the second time in less than twenty-four hours, Roz found herself staring at the back of Bailey's head in sullen silence, knowing that, for all his discretion, the chauffeur must be thoroughly intrigued by the developments in his employer's private life. Not that his face showed anything of the sort, and it stayed completely blank as he helped Roz out when they got to the house and practically handed her to James. For one farcical moment, Roz thought the two of them were going to frog-march her to the front door.

'Please wait,' James told Bailey over his shoulder, marching her into the house himself.

Roz headed straight into the drawing-room, pouncing on the bag of films with all the fervour of a mother finding her lost child.

'I'm sorry about interrupting your meeting,' she said, almost gaily, the frenetic anxiety melted away now that she had the films in her hands.

'I should hope so,' James replied coldly from the doorway. 'It was a very important meeting, and I didn't appreciate my wife bursting in like a harridan. Next time you want to come and see me, kindly let me know first.'

Roz reddened like a · schoolgirl. She had expected a casual 'Forget it,' not a humiliating reproof. Mortified, she came back at him angrily. 'Make an appointment with the efficient Ms Russell, you mean? Don't worry, there won't be a next time, I can promise you that. What was the so-important meeting about, anyway?' she asked belligerently, curious in spite of herself. There had been something about those men around the table; she could not remember their faces, and the dreadful embarrassment had made everything into a blur, yet an impression lingered in her mind that something about them had been out of character. She had met enough newspaper people in her time to sense that. 'Sorry, I didn't mean to pry,' she said hurriedly, when James didn't answer.

'We were talking takeover.' James's voice sounded strained. He was looking at her carefully, as if his answer would have some special significance for her.

'Oh, I see.' That explained the men— lawyers . . . accountants. James buying up some paper or other was nothing to get excited about, everybody seemed to be doing that these days;

the papers were full of takeover stories. Curiosity satisfied, Roz lost interest. They had never discussed James's business, and the only interest she had ever expressed was when she had discovered that Allied Press was the publisher of a couple of magazines that might possibly take some of her photographs—but that was before her photography had become such a sore point between them, and she had never mentioned it again.

'Did you have a good sleep?' James asked, coming off his high horse after a moment.

'Oh, yes, thanks. I feel a lot better.' Roz allowed a little friendliness to creep into her voice.

'Good.' James eyes did a rapid assessment of her face. 'You look a whole lot better, too. What about the reporters? They haven't been hassling you this morning, have they?'

'One or two. But I did manage to deal with them.'

James didn't miss the tartness, but chose to ignore it. 'They shouldn't bother you after today. I've seen to that.' He moved to the drinks tray set up on the chiffonier. 'Would you like a drink?' he offered hospitably.

'No, thank you,' Roz declined the offer with a polite smile, and James put the decanter down without unstopping it. He glanced at his watch. 'It's important I get back to the office, so I can't offer you lunch, I'm afraid, but what about dinner tonight?' he suggested, amazingly, as if going out to dinner was something they did every other night.

Her lips pursing automatically into a 'no', Roz had begun to shake her head before he had even finished the invitation.

Everything about James seemed to tighten. 'Why not?' he asked, retaining the careful casualness that did not fool her for a moment.

Why not? Was James stupid? Surely, if their heated exchange the previous night had shown them anything, it was how much anger still lay between them, and how impossible it was for them to be together for more than two seconds without resorting to hurling recriminations about. Telling James exactly why his invitation to dinner was an insane suggestion would plunge them headlong into a full-scale row with whys and wherefores flying. Again. Roz couldn't face it.

Ignoring the question, she said with stiff courtesy, 'Thank you, James, but no.' Swinging the bag of films over her shoulder, she walked briskly to the door.

James followed. 'What about lunch some day soon, then?'

The fatuous pretence that they were on lunching terms was too much to take. 'For heaven's sake, I said no! Not lunch, not dinner, not anything,' snapped Roz, reaching her hand to the doorknob.

Cutting across her, James's hand got there first, closing over the knob and holding the door shut. Roz glared at him.

'Why not, Rosalind?' James persisted with dogged obtuseness.

'You know damned well why not!' Roz was provoked into retorting. Then, reining in her exasperation, she let out an exaggerated sigh. 'Look, James, you've been very understanding about everything, and I appreciate it,' she said with an air of speaking to a dim child, 'but let's just leave it there, shall we?' she finished pleasantly.

She could tell from James's eyes that she couldn't have made him more furious if she'd tried. She started picking at his fingers, trying to get them off the doorknob. A mistake. With a swift twist, James's fingers closed around her wrist and held it fast.

'What are you afraid will happen if we have dinner together?' James smiled at her with soft menace.

The smile was unnerving, and so was the touch of his fingers on her skin. A nerve gone wild was pulsing madly in her throat. 'Afraid? Don't be absurd, James! It's not a matter of being afraid. It's simply pointless seeing each other again, that's all,' she managed to say with brusque nonchalance.

'That's not what your lovely grey eyes are saying. They're telling me you're very much afraid of finding yourself this close to me.'

Roz darted the giveaway eyes from his face. 'That's only because you're being so unreasonable,' she muttered, feeling a mixture of confusion and resentment that James always thought he could see right through her. He succeeded in piercing her guard just often enough to sustain his smug belief in himself. 'After last night, you know perfectly well that we've nothing more to say to each other.' She swung her eyes back to his face in hostile challenge. 'Not unless you've changed your mind and decided to be reasonable about a divorce.'

James released his hold on her wrist and almost threw her hand back at her in an abrupt, angry gesture. 'I think we've got a lot to say to each other before we start to bandy divorce about.' James gave a grim smile. 'That's your trouble, Rosalind, you dig your little heels in and refuse to talk anything through—it's just up and off with you. Well, I for one am not prepared to turn my back on what was essentially a good marriage, before we've had it out like two sensible adults.'

'Hah! Why don't you call it a perfect marriage and be done with it?' Roz suggested jeeringly. 'The trouble isn't with me, James, the trouble is with your damned ego which won't let you face the fact that your wife walked out on you twelve months ago and has no intention of coming back.'

The bitter twist of James's mouth wasn't anywhere near a smile. 'Eleven months and two weeks. Get your facts straight, Rosalind,' he corrected, and startled her with the accuracy of the trivial amendment. Had James been counting the months...the days too? It was something Roz had found herself doing willy-nilly from the day she left him—mentally ticking off the days for no particular reason other than that she couldn't help it—but it hadn't occurred to her James might have been doing the same. It was a disconcerting idea. She studied him curiously, all the time unconsciously rubbing her wrist where his fingers seemed to have left their imprint.

'I would have thought you've had sufficient time to have worked through all those bees in your bonnet and stopped carrying on with this childish game of avoiding me.' James raked his fingers roughly through his hair. 'Every time I've tried to get in touch with you, I've encountered a brick wall. You've refused to see me, refused to talk to me on the telephone, you've returned my letters—and I'm not talking just about the cheques I've tried to send you.'

It was all true, but with good reason: she had been in utter turmoil when she'd left him—scared and confused that James had put up such a fight when she had honestly believed he would be relieved their fiasco of a marriage had come to an end at last. She hadn't allowed for his ego, of course, and the safest thing had been to keep completely out of his way because, irrationally, she had been terrified that somehow James would force her to come back.

'I'm not the only one with bees in their bonnet, as you so quaintly put it,' Roz rallied, belatedly. 'If you hadn't been so pig-headed, we could have come to an amicable understanding ages ago.'

'Amicable divorce, you mean, don't you?' James shot back at her. 'I was supposed to hand you a divorce on a plate and no questions asked— just allow myself to be divorced on grounds of *my* unreasonable behaviour, as your solicitor had the nerve to put it.' James barked out an ugly laugh. 'I've no intention of doing that!'

'You don't have to rub it in. You've already made it patently clear,' returned Roz with icy anger.

'Then it's more than you've ever done. You've never made it clear—patently or otherwise—why you wanted out. Other than giving me that non-sense about career and "doing your own thing", and I don't buy that.'

Roz pounced on the taunt with self-righteous indignation. 'There you go again, right on cue—sneering about the one thing that's important to me.'

An angry red wove up James's cheeks. 'If I do, it's because you've blown it up out of proportion and let yourself become obsessive about it—shut everything else out. And everybody,' James re-taliated on a rising anger. He managed to shock her into a brief silence of utter disbelief that he could twist the facts around like that and make himself out the injured party. Or, more amaz-ingly, that he might actually believe it.

A little bitter cackle broke out of her. 'Who shut who out? Don't bother answering,' Roz hissed, recovering her anger. 'I'm not hanging around here to listen to any more insults.' And not staying around to betray herself by letting all the pent-up hurt come gushing out. She had never told him about her suspicions as to how he had spent all those nights away, never accused him of cheating on her. She had hung on to her pride and she wanted to hang on to it now.

'Goodbye, James.' Roz didn't look at him as she tore out of the room, and James made no move to stop her this time.

CHAPTER THREE

Roz had not been away for more than an hour
and a half, which meant Lyn had been kept
waiting barely half an hour—hardly a reason to
launch herself at the cab as it pulled up and hop
about, seething with impatience while Roz finished paying the fare.

'You've got them! Thank heavens for that.'
Lyn snatched up the carrier bag and danced up
the path with it ahead of Roz. 'I've been positively frantic waiting here for you—another
minute and I swear I was going to break down
the door in case you were skulking inside because
you actually *had* lost the films and were too
chicken to tell me.'

In spite of her bad temper, Roz had to laugh.
In her thirties, Lyn Barrett was barely five feet
and as slight as a sparrow; she would have been
hard pressed to break through a cardboard
carton, let alone put a dent in a thick wooden
door.

Lyn's green eyes narrowed into slits under the
crop of orange fringe as she grinned at the pre-
posterousness of her own threat, but once inside
the sitting-room the grin came off and Lyn didn't
waste a moment getting down to business. Un-
zipping the bag, she poured out its contents on
to the sofa and made a rapid tally of the rolls of

film and then still had to ask, anxiously, 'You didn't lose any?'

'All there. Probably too many, if anything,' Roz assured her.

'Never too many. It's best to take more than you need—gives you more choice when it comes to making the selection. I'm for ever dinning that into my students.'

Roz watched her finger the rolls caressingly and felt a twinge of resentment. Just as she had predicted to herself, Lyn's first concern was for the films, and it had not yet occurred to her to ask after Roz's experience.

Roz gave a mental shrug and tried not to mind. Lyn was Lyn and, while she might not be the most sensitive of people, she had been there when Roz had needed her after leaving James. Lyn had given her a roof over her head for two months until Roz found her feet—and the flat—and through Lyn's photographic agency which she ran with her friend Peter, she had put quite a number of jobs Roz's way—jobs Roz certainly would not have had the confidence to apply for at the time, when she was so insecure about everything she was ready to believe she was having herself on about her 'damned-fool hobby'. Lyn had blithely pushed her into each job with an 'of course you can do it,' and, remarkably, Roz *had* been able to do it, her self-assurance growing in leaps and bounds. Until the Zangyrian assignment.

'You weren't really kidnapped, were you?' Lyn gave her a quick, birdlike glance. 'Thought not,' she said dismissively as Roz shook her head. 'I rang the Famine Relief people and they told me it was some mix-up or other. That's what being a photographer is all about—things happen to you. You must have got some super shots.' The wistfulness was like a child's. 'Wish I'd been there.'

'You'd have been welcome to it,' Roz snapped a little. 'Coffee?' Without waiting for an answer, she went into the kitchen, feeling let down that Lyn was making so light of something Roz had found so dreadful, and frustrated that she couldn't talk to Lyn about it because Lyn would think her an idiot. Or worse, unprofessional.

She came back with two mugs of black instant coffee, scraped out from the bottom of the jar. 'I haven't got anything else to offer you, there's nothing in the place. I'll have to go down the street and do some shopping later if I don't want to starve to death,' she added in a thoughtless aside and made herself flinch. 'At least I have a choice in the matter. Others should be so lucky...' Roz muttered, handing Lyn the coffee.

Lyn took the mug and took a long, hard look at Roz as she did it. 'You seem a bit uptight. Anything the matter?' she asked, and Roz felt a quiver of slightly hysterical laughter at the in- genuousness of the question.

'I'm just tired, I guess. It's all been rather a strain.' She gave a tight smile. 'What with one thing and another,' she said without elaborating, and thought, take your pick—famine, guerillas, James.

Lyn nodded sagely, making the light dance off the outrageously bright cap of hair. 'Some jobs can be like that—get under your skin for a while. I shouldn't let it worry you,' she advised with the closest thing to sympathy, or perhaps understanding, that Roz had ever heard from her. 'Anyway, it will all have been worth it once I get these printed, you'll see.' Lyn tapped the bag beside her, gently, then frowned. 'Lord only knows how I'll manage to get them printed in time. You've lost us the best part of a week you know, and the Relief mob's fund-raising caper is in ten days. Doesn't give me much time.' Reverting to her usual thoughtlessness, she made it sound as if the time lost in getting back to England was the result of a capricious whim on Roz's part, then, surprisingly quickly—for Lyn—she realised how she must have sounded. 'Sorry, Roz, I know it's not your fault and that it must have been awful for you. I know what,' Lyn went on, brightening, 'why don't you came and stay with me for a day or so until you...'

'Oh, not you, too!' Roz reacted with a sharpness that took her by surprise. 'No. Thanks, anyway,' she muttered ungraciously. 'I'm OK and I'll be fine here.'

Lyn didn't look the least put out by Roz's reaction to her invitation; she looked intrigued. 'Who's been issuing unwelcome invitations before me, then?' she asked facetiously, eyes alert with curiosity.

Roz wasn't going to tell her but, knowing Lyn would periwinkle it out of her some way or another, said shortly, 'James, if you must know.'

The ginger eyebrows shot up into the thatch of fringe. 'Well, well! I wondered what was up when I spotted his thunderous face at your side on the telly last night, but didn't like to ask. Is that where you were last night? His place? I didn't realise you two were back on such amiable terms again.'

'We're not!' snapped Roz as her face stupidly went hot. 'And anyway, it's not your business.'

There was a heavy little silence in which Roz almost apologised but didn't because she was just too irritated by Lyn and her insatiable curiosity.

Lyn abruptly got up from the sofa, lifting the carrier bag in the same movement. 'I'll give you a ring when I have the prints done, and we can select the ones for the fund-raising,' she said briskly, assuming the role of the agent that she was, making an arrangement with one of her photographers. 'I'll see myself out.' Terribly businesslike and highly miffed, she marched out without waiting for Roz to see her to the door.

Roz let out her frustration in a sigh. What was the matter with her? Her temper and nerves were hanging precariously by a thread, stretched and ready to snap the moment anyone opened their mouths. Lyn was not renowned for her tact, and her curiosity was second to none, but that was no excuse to bite her head off.

The trouble was, Lyn had touched dangerous ground. James was a taboo subject between them

and had been that way for ages—the result of too
many confidences shared earlier in their
friendship, when, never having had a close
woman friend before, Roz had found herself
telling Lyn all sorts of things about James and
the marriage—things that should have remained
private between herself and James. It was a be-
trayal in a way, which Roz soon regretted and
clammed up, and Lyn eventually stopped making
derogatory comments about James in particular,
and chauvinistic husbands in general. She'd had
one herself once—before her single-mindedness
about her work had edged 'what's-his-name' out
of her life, or so Roz had deduced from Lyn's
airy dismissal of her erstwhile marriage. Her attitude quite shocked Roz and made her wonder
whether in five years or so she was going to feel
as blithely indifferent to James as Lyn was to the
hapless 'what's-his-name'.

Roz took the mugs into the kitchen, then went
off to the local shopping centre to withdraw some
cash at the bank and buy in some basic supplies
to tide her over for a couple of days. On the way
back, she got caught at the gate by the woman
next door. That was all she needed, Roz thought
in irritation. The woman was thrilled to bits at
having read about Roz in the papers, and was
avid for gory details. Such was fame—a
neighbour hanging over the fence to nab you so
she could tell her friends she'd spoken to you,
thought Roz sourly. While she was tersely polite,
she was too annoyed to be amused and managed
to escape with a few non-committal comments

which must have sent her new status as the local celebrity plummeting behind her.

In a worse mood than when she had gone out, Roz put away the purchases and walked out into the tiny patch of struggling lawn that masqueraded as a backyard, and mooched about, restless and on edge, wondering what to do with herself. The sky was clouding over in a desultory fashion, as if it couldn't make up its mind whether to threaten rain or not. Roz wished it would; a good downpour might get rid of some of the tension inside her. Or a good sleep.

She wandered back inside and went to bed, and then it seemed that for the next three days all she did was sleep, not leaving the flat once, but scratching up bitsy snacks from the meagre supplies she had bought, and staring unseeingly at the television once or twice, but mainly sleeping.

Yet, for all the time in bed, she didn't feel much better. The tension had ironed itself out into a sort of dull flatness, verging on apathy, when even making herself a cup of coffee required a mammoth effort, and answering the telephone was beyond her whether she was up or not. Roz couldn't work out what was wrong with her.

Was she having a nervous breakdown? She considered the idea and laughed it off—grimly; but, really disturbed by her inexplicable state of withdrawal and indifference, forced herself to answer the telephone the next time it rang.

She might have known it would be Lyn. 'Where on earth have you been?' Lyn demanded without preliminaries. 'My finger is ready to drop off

from all the dialling I've done! You might at least
have let me know the other day that you wouldn't
be staying at the flat.' The insinuation was that
Roz had gone off to stay with James; Roz
couldn't be bothered correcting it.

'I've been out a bit...' Like a light, she could
have added. 'Sorry I missed you. What is it?'

'What is it, the woman asks?' Lyn feigned astonishment and in the next breath almost
shrieked, 'Roz, they're fantastic! I've rushed the
prints through, and they're marvellous. Absolutely terrific!' Lyn's wild enthusiasm threatened
damage to Roz's eardrum.

She pulled the phone back its mandatory inches
and said dully, 'Oh!' The onslaught of superla-
tives was too much to take in. Lyn had paused,
presumably to give Roz the chance to shriek back
in delight. 'Do you think the Famine Relief
people will like them?' Roz asked uncertainly.
They were the ones paying for the job—a fact
Lyn was apt to overlook.

'Are you crazy? The photos will tear the hearts
out of anybody who sees them; wallets will be
jumping out of pockets. The Relief mob will love
them—they'll be mad if they don't,' Lyn bellowed at her with vehement sincerity. 'Truly, Roz,
they're great. Come right over and see for
yourself.'

'Now?'

'What's the matter with now?' Lyn demanded
impatiently. 'You're not doing anything at the
moment, are you? Come for lunch, why don't
you?'

'No. Yes. Yes, all right, I'll come for lunch,' Roz agreed unenthusiastically. Lunches at Lyn's tended towards collections of crackers past their freshness and bits and pieces of hard cheese. After Roz's own unappetising diet of the last three days, the invitation to lunch was not the carrot Lyn thought she was dangling to get Roz over to Surrey.

'Good.' Lyn rang off abruptly, and Roz just stood there, holding the receiver in her hand.

It must be true; Lyn didn't dole out praise lightly. She was a superb photographer herself and an absolute tyrant in her standards where her agency's reputation was concerned.

Somewhere underneath the flatness, Roz supposed there was some part of her that must be pleased. Perhaps when she saw the prints for herself a little of Lyn's excitement might rub off on her, and the sense of nightmare about the whole Zangyrian project would go away.

Roz put the phone down and set about getting herself ready. She was still in the dressing-gown she had virtually been living in for three days, and needed a bath before she could get dressed. At her slow, dulled pace, it took a full hour before she was ready to leave, and then the phone rang again. Roz hesitated, then answered it on the off chance it was Lyn, ringing to say don't come after all. She instantly regretted it.

'Hello, Rosalind.' James was low-key casual.

Roz ground her teeth in a grimace. 'What do you want, James?' she snapped discouragingly. 'I'm busy, so make it quick.'

'I've been trying to get on to you for the last two days,' James went on as if she hadn't spoken.

'Join the queue,' Roz muttered tartly. 'I asked you what you wanted, didn't you hear me?'

She visualised James's face seizing up into a scowl but the voice in her ear stayed pleasant. 'I wanted to apologise if I said anything to upset you the other day.' The sincerity came over very strongly—easily done over the telephone, without your face to give you away.

Suspect James's motive though she did, Roz couldn't bring herself to snarl at someone offering an apology, and in the short moment she was stumped for a comeback James went on in a slight hurry, as if he was expecting her to hang up on him. 'Please have lunch with me today, Rosalind. There really is something I'd like to discuss with you.'

There it was again—that obtuse, unreasonable persistence. 'But there's nothing I want to discuss with you, James. I think we've said everything we have to say to each other. If you've had second thoughts about the divorce, see your solicitor. Now, if you don't mind, I'm really very busy,' she finished with mock politeness. 'I'm overdue at Lyn's to view my prints as it is,' she added, and could have kicked herself for volunteering the gratuitous information. Why give James a reason? She didn't owe him any explanations.

'Has she done them already?' James's voice perked up. 'That was quick.'

'Yes.'

'Then let me drive you over there. It'll save you some time,' James offered, and must have thought her an idiot.

'No, thank you. Goodbye, James.' Roz hung up quickly, but without slamming the telephone down in his ear, which would have given away how much even talking to him over a telephone rattled her. Given the state of her nerves, she'd have felt safer taking a swim with a shark than accepting a lift from James, who gave her the uneasy sense of circling around, closing in on her and ready to pounce the moment she weakened. A shark, yes; didn't they circle their victims first?

Lyn's ancient little car was parked at its usual careless angle at the side of the cottage as Roz came up the lane from the station. The other car, very neatly parked in the drive, she recognised as Peter's, Lyn's friend and partner in their photographic agency. Peter was the business mind behind the venture, Lyn the creative talent, and together they made a formidable duo, specialising in rather off-beat assignments and up-and-coming young photographers. While unorthodox, and outside the mainstream agencies, they were very 'picky', and Roz was grateful, not to say flattered, to be on their books.

The front door was open—it invariably was—but no one answered her knock or her call. Letting herself in, Roz greeted the umpteen cats that always seemed to find a home at Lyn's, and walked straight through the cottage and out into the back garden, where Lyn had had a studio complex built some years ago to house studio, showroom, darkroom and a cluttered room that was the agency's office.

Lyn's laughter pealed out through an open window as Roz reached the square, unprepossessing brick structure which was eventually to be hidden by a cover of ivy—or so Lyn hoped. She walked in without knocking. Lyn must have just darted into the studio or darkroom, because there were only the two men in the showroom—mini-gallery, Peter liked to call it. They were bending over a table at the far end of the room, and both looked up as Roz entered and stayed frozen a step inside the door.

James smiled. 'Since I couldn't give you a lift up here, I thought you might like one back,' he said, super-casually, while his eyes fixed on her hostile face in wary expectation of her next move.

For a long moment, Roz was not sure what that move was going to be—turn on her heel and stomp off, or let fly at James—and embarrass the life out of Peter, who might not have known what the instant charge of tension was all about, but certainly knew it was there. He had the look of someone who wished he was anywhere but where he was.

He was a slight, wispy young man with a perpetually worried air about him that belied a basically cheerful personality. Roz liked him.

'Hello, Peter,' she greeted him with a smile that was possibly a little too brilliant for the occasion, and which very pointedly did not include James. 'Nice to see you.'

Peter relaxed visibly, giving a rather silly grin in his relief and murmuring something Roz didn't catch, because at that moment Lyn came bouncing in through the door behind them and spotted Roz.

'Oh good, you're here! What are you doing just standing there? The prints are over on that table.' She flapped a hand towards James and Peter. 'But I've done some blow-ups already. Come and take a look at them first.' Lyn bounded to the side wall, where a number of screens were permanently set up to accommodate recent and current examples of their agency's talent.

Without another glance at James, Roz went over to Lyn at the screen. 'What is he doing here?' she hissed in an undertone.

Lyn tossed her a blank look. Roz jerked an angry shoulder, and then gave several jerks of the head in James's direction, where he and Peter had returned to their examination of the prints on the table and were talking between themselves.

Lyn squinted in a puzzled frown before her face cleared and she understood what Roz's pantomime had been about. 'But didn't you ask him here?'

'Of course I didn't!' Roz glared at her.

'But he said...'

'Oh, forget it,' Roz muttered in suppressed rage. She could guess what James had said—or implied—something about having arranged to meet her here to see the prints, or to pick her up, or whatever. What did it matter? He was here now, and all she could do was ignore him—for the moment. Later, she would allow herself the luxury of explosion. How dared James ride rough-shod over her refusal to see her, and foist himself on her—and so damned deviously, at that.

'I thought it was your idea to have him here,' Lyn started to explain in a penetrating whisper that rose above the muted conversation of the two men.

'I said, forget it,' Roz repeated through clenched teeth.

Lyn shrugged. 'OK, but I want you to know it wasn't my idea. Anyway, he's awfully impressed by your stuff,' she couldn't resist saying, pleased, and sounding as if she was giving James a pat on the head. Much could be forgiven if you weren't a complete philistine, that was Lyn's way of looking at things.

Not Roz's. But her fury would keep.

'Come on, let's look,' Lyn urged her. 'You haven't even glanced at them yet.'

Roz moved in front of the first screen and stared in silence.

'What did I tell you?' Lyn breathed excitedly at her side. 'Super! I'll do the exhibition ones a good deal larger than that—poster-size, I think—with one or two really enormous ones for backdrops, or whatever they want to use them for.'

Oblivious of Roz's lack of response, Lyn prattled on, darting from one screen to another and back again, while Roz stood still, everything and everybody in the room disappearing from her consciousness, a knot tightening in her chest at what she was seeing in front of her. Her mind did a flip and catapulted her back into all the dreadfulness she had so recently left behind, and which, in a sort of emotional self-defence, she had somehow managed to keep pushed back in some deep recess of her brain.

Now as everything sprang forward, they were here with her, in front of her—the strangely silent crowd of pitiful, ragged people waiting behind a wire fence at the perimeter of the dusty airstrip, or rather, the levelled-out piece of ground that passed for one. The shot was from the bottom of the plane's steps. Roz's heart had stopped at the sight that had confronted her then, but her professional instincts must have taken over, because she had no recollection of taking the photograph.

She peeled her eyes away, and across Lyn's screen the anonymous crowd zoomed into close-ups—women, children, old men, their eyes without exception were dark wells of haunting hopelessness. It was unbearable, but Roz made herself look.

'Taking some in black and white was a brilliant idea. It gives a sharper definition to the faces, although you don't get quite the same sense of the heat and isolation as you do with colour—all to do with light, of course.' Lyn switched into lecturer mode.

Roz had been nervous she would run out of film, and had bought some back-up rolls in one of the bigger towns. Black and white was all that had been available; the last thing on her mind had been to use those suffering faces to play technical games with light and shade. Roz wanted to hit Lyn. To cry. She blinked hard, holding herself rigid to keep control.

James and Peter had come over to the screen and, without turning her head, Roz knew James was standing very close behind her.

Lyn was pointing to a shot of a young woman who had scarcely passed girlhood; she was holding a baby tightly to herself as they sat on the ground a little apart from a nearby group. 'There's a really interesting feel to that one, Roz... the way you've captured her own private sense of isolation. I rather think you'd be well in the running for an award if you entered it in a competition somewhere. What do you think, Peter?'

Whatever thoughts Peter might have had on the matter didn't get voiced, because Roz's control snapped in that moment. She spun on Lyn, who took a hasty, startled step away from her. 'If it takes a dead baby and a grieving mother to win an award, then I hope to God I never win one!'

Eyes blurred and tears streaming uncontrollably down her cheeks, Roz pushed blindly past Lyn and dashed from the studio, across the garden and out of the cottage, her only conscious thought to get away from those unbearable images, and from Lyn's bright, uncaring analysis of them. How Lyn could look at them and talk dispassionately of angles, sharp definition and other such claptrap was incredible to Roz. And grotesque.

She was already half-way down the lane before she became aware of her surroundings and slowed down her furious pace. Then, on hearing a train, she broke into a run again, reaching the station as the train pulled in. One last dash got her into it before it started off again.

Breathless and winded by the pain in her chest, Roz subsided into a seat, avoiding the odd stare of curiosity cast in her direction, and not caring anyway what the occupants of the carriage thought of the tear-stained, dishevelled young woman who had come pelting in as if all the devils of hell were at her heels. She knew what James and the others were thinking—that she had taken leave of her senses—and they were right, since there wasn't any other explanation for her fit of hysteria.

By the time she'd changed trains for the underground trip home, Roz felt better, and she walked the last stretch from the station wrapped in a tight, careful calmness, until her eyes picked up the navy Porsche outside the house. A moment later, her brain registered what her eyes were seeing: James's private car, and apparently the object of admiration or simple envy of the gathering of local youths—trainee thugs eyeing it from the kerb on the opposite side of the road.

James eased himself out of the car as Roz approached. She had had about thirty yards' grace to get her lines together to tell him to go to hell but, reaching him, it all seemed too much of a waste of breath to translate her thoughts into words. Roz looked through him and turned into her gate without a word. James caught up with her at the front door.

'Go away, James. Leave me alone,' Roz said wearily, not expecting him to listen to her for a moment, and not putting up any protest when he followed her into the hall, since the alternative was a stand-up row on the doorstep, or possibly being bundled ignominiously indoors like a recalcitrant child.

She let both of them into her flat. 'Make yourself at home, why don't you?' she said sarcastically. As she said it, she realised this was James's first time in her flat, and realised too that it was the last sort of place he would want to make his home. After what James was used to, her present home wouldn't rate much above a hovel with him!

Put out by the thought, Roz left him standing in the corridor and marched straight off to the bathroom, shutting the door on him. Going over to the washbasin, she took a look into the mirror above it and nearly died.

There was a stony gauntness about her face that made her look about a hundred; her mouth was clamped into a tight, grim line; the eyes were slightly puffed, with reddish rims around them from the crying. Horrified, Roz quickly splashed her face with cold water, then dampened the face-flannel and pressed it against her swollen lids for a few moments. On an afterthought, she dabbed on some lipstick and ran a comb through her hair before pulling it back into its ponytail again.

She found James in the kitchen, in the act of closing the refrigerator door as she came in. 'I didn't mean for you to make yourself at home quite so literally,' Roz told him with tart resentment.

James took in her attempt to tidy herself up in a long, careful look, but didn't make any comment on it. 'I've just been through your cupboards. You haven't a scrap of food in the house.'

'I didn't know I was supposed to be running a restaurant! You should have booked if you wanted a meal,' Roz retorted, swinging her back on him, and going into the sitting-room. She took off her jacket and threw it on to the sofa.

James came out of the kitchen, glanced at the jacket, then picked it up and held it out to her. 'You can put this right back on, Rosalind. We're going out. To eat. It's obvious you haven't had a decent meal since you returned from Zangyria, and it's telling on you.'

Roz ignored the proffered jacket. 'I haven't been hungry,' she muttered, not bothering to deny his accusation. 'And, anyway, it's not your business.' She had been saying that a lot lately— to Lyn, reporters, her father...Now James. Everybody, it appeared, had latched on to the idea that they were entitled to stick their noses into her business.

'What, in heaven's name, are you doing to yourself?' James came back at her in a burst of angry frustration. He took a step towards her,

her jacket in his hand, then stopped and looked at her strangely. 'Are you trying to starve yourself out of misguided guilt for the misery you saw in Zangyria? That's it, isn't it?' He nodded slowly, satisfied with his crazy conclusion.

'Don't be absurd!' Roz said quickly, a little shocked. It was crazy, but could it be true? Was that what her inexplicable behaviour of the last three days was all about?

'Not me, Rosalind. It's you who's wearing yourself down into a breakdown. Have you taken a good look at yourself? You've lost at least half a stone in the last couple of days, and it's small wonder you're not coping with whatever is going on inside your head.' James put her jacket over her shoulder. 'Well, you're coming out to eat with me now, if I have to carry you and force-feed you when we get there!'

CHAPTER FOUR

THEY had come to one of those ubiquitous, characterless chain eateries that had sprung up in practically every shopping centre, their only vague claim to recommendation being that they served meals any time of the day and most of the night.

Roz had been hungry, but she had come with James more from fright than the promise of a square meal. James was no psychologist, but he had given her the jolt she needed, his comment setting off a few nasty alarm bells in her head, and she wasn't so stupid that she wasn't concerned about her strange disinclination to eat.

The meal was eaten in silent, isolated concentration, almost as if they were strangers forced to share a table in a crowded restaurant; only, at four o'clock, the place was virtually deserted and they were certainly not strangers. Now, with the self-absorbing activity of eating out of the way, Roz took her first sip of coffee, bracing herself for James to pick up where he'd left off giving his penny's worth of potted psychology. She looked across the table at him, half curious as to how far he would try to go, but knowing that, one way or another, he would be harking back to their marriage, her career, her refusal to discuss reconciliation; like a dog with a favourite old bone, she thought tiredly.

Roz sighed inside as James opened his mouth to speak; the truce was over.

'I never told you what happened to me after I returned from my first assignment in Beirut, did I?' James asked conversationally. With the cup at her lips, Roz looked at him over the rim in checked surprise. On guard though she was, she could not recognise James's opening gambit as a lead-in to what she was expecting. She put the cup down and, treating the question as rhetorical, said nothing.

'Well, it was about twelve years ago, and I'd just come down from Cambridge and joined the staff of one of Dad's newspapers as a reporter.' Like an old bore at a cocktail party, James determinedly went on in the face of her lack of encouragement. 'It was my first real assignment, and I was as bright-eyed and bushy-tailed as they came, and champing at the bit to make a success of it. I had great hopes of making a name for myself as a political reporter at the time. Overnight, of course.' James's mouth twisted into a self-deprecatory smile at the memory. Roz couldn't picture him at all. 'The troubles in Beirut had already been going for a number of years; I'd heard about them, read about them and seen those dreadful pictures on television, but nothing quite prepares you for the real thing, does it?' James looked at her steadily.

Roz was listening hard, but looked back almost blankly as she began to understand the direction James's story was going to take.

'I was inside a nearby building when a car bomb went off in the street. The explosion was enough in itself to scare me witless,' James continued with a casual chattiness, 'but then, like the good reporter I hoped to be, I pulled myself together and bounded out for my first-hand story.' The casualness cut off mid-air. James turned away abruptly, a stricken look on his face. When he brought his eyes back to her after a moment, his voice had taken on a brittle hardness. 'A young woman, a couple of toddlers and a young boy—all in various stages of mutilation. Funny thing,' James ran on quickly after the appalling tally, 'I was OK at the time. It was only after being home for about a week that I went to pieces. Drank myself stupid for weeks, trying to blot it all out.'

Roz felt her shock washing over her in wave after disturbing wave as the impact of the glossed-over story hit home. 'And did you?' she asked softly, her mind not quite able to associate the emotionally distraught young reporter with the picture of her husband as she had always known him: cool, self-assured, always in control of himself, and usually everybody around him. The point of James's story was too obvious to miss, but that he was prepared to expose his vulnerability like this was something else. He was telling her that he, too, had emotional feet of clay. Like anybody else. Like Roz herself.

James was shaking his head at her. 'Trying to blot it out was a mistake, and the drinking only made it worse. What I needed was to talk about it. Cry about it. I did in the end—to Cecily, bless her. It did take a while, but eventually those massacred bodies left off burning a hole inside my head night and day, and amazingly even those poor kids stopped haunting me, too. I never thought they would...could...'

'I know, I know!' Roz suddenly interrupted in a helpless whisper. 'It was the children in Zangyria, too...all those children. Everything was so awful, but it was seeing them and not being able to do anything that was the worst part—and having to go around and take those damned photographs.' Roz gave an involuntary shudder. 'It made me feel unspeakable.'

She started to raise the cup, but her hand was not up to the task; it shook alarmingly and she put the cup down again with a jarring clatter, then went to drop the hand to her lap. But James reached across the table and took hold of it, keeping it on top of the table, clasped firmly in his. Roz did not attempt to withdraw it. 'Tell me more,' he ordered gently, and she did.

Week after week of repressed misery came pouring out in a harsh, painful torrent; once the floodgates opened, Roz couldn't stop herself, going through village by ravaged village and reliving three weeks of what, to her, had been a waking nightmare, and ending with the mistaken abduction. 'I was so scared. So, so scared,' she finished, dabbing at her eyes with her free hand.

So what did it matter if James knew what a panic-stricken, miserable little kid she had reverted to when it came to the test? His own confession had rendered keeping up a front no longer important to her pride; that was how James meant it to be. Roz tried to smile. 'Well, that's the whole sorry story.' The attempt at a smile didn't come off and neither did the facetiousness: her voice was shaky and a little hoarse from the talking and emotion. Looking down, Roz saw their hands, fingers entwined on the table, and glanced up nonplussed, not remembering how they came to be like that. With an embarrassed tug, she freed her hand and then just sat there, staring at it.

James must have signalled to the waitress for more coffee, because she came and took the stone-cold ones away and replaced them with fresh ones. Roz sipped hers in silence.

James took a preoccupied sip of his, then set his cup down and met her eyes in a steady gaze. 'You mustn't let one painful experience affect how you feel about your work. You produced a very fine collection of photographs under awful conditions. I was impressed,' he said, almost stiltedly, giving the impression he had put each word together with great care.

Her work was such a sore point between them that, in spite of this unexpected truce, Roz's defences sprang to the alert as she tried to read some cleverly camouflaged disparagement in James's comment, and couldn't. Her eyes searched his face for any telltale sign at variance with the sincerity of carefully chosen words, but could find nothing in the frank gaze either. In the end, Roz muttered, 'Thanks,' and coloured a little at how ungracious she sounded.

James's wry smile told her he knew how much it cost her to accept the compliment. 'I meant what I said, and I've seen the work of enough professional photographers to judge—and so has your friend Lyn. You've got talent, Rosalind; you must know that yourself.'

She did, and there had been moments, even entire assignments, when she felt so good about her work that she was on an absolute high, when nothing seemed more fulfilling or important in her life than the job on hand. And yet it had taken only one negative experience like the Zangyrian assignment to send her into shockwaves of doubt—not about the talent Roz honestly believed she had, but whether she had the necessary detachment to develop into a really top-class professional. Or the commitment. Or, if it came to the crunch, whether she really wanted to acquire them and be like . . . Lyn?

Roz gave herself a quick mental shake and forced an outward smile that gave no hint of what had been going on inside her head. 'Thanks for the vote of confidence. Sorry if I sounded churlish—old habits and all that,' she put in drily. 'Can we go now?' Roz picked up her handbag and stood up rather hastily, conscious of the subtle danger in sitting there exchanging confidences over coffee like two old friends—which they were not. Giving in and telling James about Zangyria was one thing; telling him of the gnawing doubts about her chosen career was another.

Roz walked ahead and waited at the door while James went to pay the bill at the cash register— no settling one's bill at the table here and, from the cashier's attitude, men like James were obviously not in the regular line of customers. Roz watched the limp-looking young woman come to life as she smiled at something James said when he handed her the money.

One eye-to-eye smile, a couple of inconsequential words, and the cashier suddenly was a woman reacting to a very attractive man and, curiously, looking more vivacious and attractive herself in those few lit-up moments. Roz had seen it happen before. The woman would cease to exist for James the moment he turned his back on her, yet it was quite likely that his careless dollop of charm had made her dreary day. Some men had it so easy, it was cruel!

'Why were you looking at me like that just then?' James asked as they went out into the street.

'Like what?'

'Like...' James shrugged. 'I'm not sure. Disapproving, I think, for want of a better word.'

She really must try to do something about letting her thoughts show in her face when James was around, thought Roz, and brushed the comment off with a small laugh. 'I was miles away, thinking,' she fibbed.

They had left the Porsche at the flat, and had walked the two blocks to the restaurant in tense,

angry silence. Walking home, they were silent
again, yet this time there was a vague com-
panionship between them. It was too fragile to
last, but Roz was conscious of wanting to hang
on to it for as long as possible.

They walked side by side, close but not
touching, until they had to cross the street and
James took her elbow. Then, instead of releasing
it on the other side of the road, he slipped her
arm through his. To her own surprise, Roz left
it there and they walked on like that, presenting
an illusion of an affectionate couple strolling
home. Like old times. The irony of it struck her
and hurt a little.

They used to take a lot of walks together. In
the early days of their relationship, it had surprised her that a man like James should enjoy
something as simple and unsophisticated as a
walk as much as she did. In her mind, the James
Thorntons of the world belonged to cocktail bars
and trendy parties, not the country lanes tucked
behind quaint old farmhouses outside the village.
Later, in London during those fifteen happy
months, they had walked the parks on Sunday
afternoons or summer evenings after James had
come home from work. Often, they had walked
in silence, holding hands, not needing to talk.
And that was the difference. They were silent now
because they did not know how to talk to each
other any more.

The collection of young louts loitering on the
opposite kerb had thinned to three or four when
she and James reached the flat. 'You had better

check they haven't stripped your car of its engine while your back was turned,' Roz said, smiling at James as she disengaged her arm.

'I'll scalp the little terrors if they've so much as laid a grubby finger on it,' James threatened with a chuckle, and put on a performance of narrowing his eyes to slits and glowering ferociously across at the kids, who didn't take the slightest bit of notice.

Roz laughed, then, with their amusement dying away, they stood awkwardly facing each other at the gate.

'Would you like to come in for coffee?' Roz heard herself make the startling offer and wondered whether she heard right.

James shook his head. 'I'd like to very much, but I'm due back at the office. I've been AWOL all afternoon as it is. It's not important,' James hastily added as Roz instantly looked uncomfortable.

'I'm sorry,' she mumbled, only just realising she was responsible for keeping James from his business, and that she had been so wrapped up in her own misery that she had simply accepted James's time without questioning it, needing his shoulder to cry on more than she'd realised. She felt chastened and very grateful, but it seemed impossibly difficult to tell James that. Words chased themselves around in her head while they continued to stand there, each seeming to wait for the other to make some move.

'James, I...' Roz flicked her tongue over her dry lips. 'I just wanted to say...' she started again, and never finished. Her eyes stayed fixed on James's mouth as he brought it slowly down to her lips. A part of her mind had known what was about to happen, and there had been time to turn her head quickly so his lips would have merely brushed her cheek, and that would have been that—a casual goodbye peck, meaning nothing in particular.

Perhaps James had intended his kiss to be nothing more than that, because, as her lips parted and Roz kissed him back with a sudden hard intensity, she sensed his momentary surprise before he cupped his hands around her face and deepened the kiss, but only for a moment, dropping his hands almost immediately and drawing his mouth away at the same time. Roz dropped her eyes in confusion as from somewhere across the road came several amateurish attempts at wolf-whistles.

'There's something I wanted to talk to you about, Rosalind,' James said urgently, as if he was afraid she was about to bolt. And Roz would have if her mind hadn't been in such a riot at what she had just done. 'I did have a reason for trying to catch you at Lyn's this afternoon.'

Roz jerked her head up. She had forgotten all about his unwelcome appearance at Lyn's studio. At the time, she had assumed he had turned up to carry on pestering her into a lunch or dinner, or merely to annoy her for the sake of it. 'What reason?' she asked, puzzled and on guard.

'Cecily.'

'Cecily?' Roz repeated like a startled parrot.

'Yes. It's her birthday on Monday. I know you've had too much on your plate to give it a thought yet,' James put in tactfully as the guilty 'Oh, God' escaped from Roz's lips, 'but Cecily asked me especially to ask you to come to see her with me when I go up this Sunday. That's what I wanted to talk to you about, but I didn't want to do it over the telephone.'

Roz was shaking her head agitatedly. 'I can't go, James. You know I can't, and it's not fair of Cecily to ask. I'll send some flowers.' She resorted inadequately to the ever-ready cop-out and saw James's jaw tighten perceptibly. 'Please be reasonable, James,' Roz pleaded. 'I'm very fond of your mother, and I promise I'll go up to see her soon, but not just yet. I must go in now, and you should be at the office.' She flicked him a nervous smile.

'Will you at least think about it and give me a definite answer? Say, on Friday, if I give you a ring then?'

'Yes, yes, all right,' Roz nodded, capitulating—she didn't know why. Because James had been so nice? Because she was in such a tizz, she didn't know what she was saying or doing? 'Goodbye, James.' She turned and fled up the path.

It took her all evening of rationalisation before she could neatly relegate her response to James's kiss to the 'so what' basket: she had been overwrought for most of the afternoon, James had been extraordinarily kind and supportive, and all her part in the kiss had amounted to was an appreciative thank you. Granted, it had gone a little too far, but it was no big deal and she was not going to torment herself making an issue out of it.

In the morning, her first waking thought was of James and the achingly familiar feel of his mouth on hers, and all the rationalisation of the previous night took on a resoundingly hollow ring. Disturbed, Roz got up and, dressing quickly, went to the kitchen and put the kettle on, then stood staring moodily out the window above the sink. The neighbour's cat was sunning itself in the corner of the yard by the fence and, as Roz watched, it yawned, stretching with the luxurious sensuality that was the feline trademark. A mindless sensuality, Roz had always thought it, and found it rather distasteful; the leg of a table or a human finger stroking it under the chin would bring on exactly the same sensual satisfaction. Cats were not particular where their pleasure was concerned.

Roz turned away from the window to turn off the kettle. Who was she to criticise cats, when her own response to James's kiss had not been any less mindless? She had reacted as if she had been starved for the touch of a man's lips. But not any man's—James's. And that was what made it so awful, because now James would start reading all sorts of things into that response. All the wrong things—he would think that she was still attracted to him, still vulnerable. And, even if she was, Roz conceded reluctantly in the face of the obvious, it was only on the physical level.

James was a very attractive man, and women responded to him; she wasn't the only one. The stab that followed that sour little thought caught her by surprise.

Jealous? Who, me? Roz mocked herself, shaking by the bitterness the idea of James with other women could still evoke. Surely she was through with all that? What James did and who he did it with was his business and couldn't affect her any more, and the last thing she needed now was to get involved with him again. If one kiss could set her off balance like this, she should take the warning and stay out of James's way, as she had done for most of the past year. Going to Cecily's with him would be an act of premeditated idiocy.

She would go alone, Roz resolved, later. Perhaps Monday or, if not then, then definitely some day during the coming week. She felt dreadfully guilty about the way she had avoided keeping in touch with her mother-in-law. Cecily was kindness itself, and had never once said a word of reproach about the breakdown of the marriage—unlike Roz's father, who thought Roz had gone out of her mind in leaving James, and didn't mince his words telling her so. Yet, while her father made her furious, a few minutes' chat with Cecily left Roz feeling rotten—about leaving James, about herself, about getting hung-up on her career, and practically everything else in between. Unreasonable, irrational, but that was how it was, and in the end it had become easier not to telephone the old lady at all. The coward's way out.

Roz started as the telephone shrilled from the sitting-room. She let it ring for ages before finally going to answer it, her mug of coffee in her hand. 'Yes?' she said warily, thinking it might be James already, and not feeling quite up to trying to tell him that she definitely wouldn't be coming with him on Sunday.

'Hello, Roz, it's Peter.' There was a distinct wariness in Peter's voice, too, which a moment later Roz put down to the remains of his embarrassment at having witnessed her impromptu show of hysteria the day before.

'Oh, hello, Peter! How are you? What can I do for you?' Roz was positively effusive in her relief that it wasn't James.

'Are you OK?' was the closest Peter's reserve would allow him as a reference to yesterday's histrionics. 'Listen, Roz,' he rushed on before she could come back with the standard trite response. 'I didn't get a chance to speak to you yesterday about that next job of yours—the travel books ... I wanted to tell you that the publisher has been on my back about it these last few weeks while you've been away. They're getting anxious to get you together with the author to work out the preliminary details, so I told them you'd come by and see them Friday—that's tomorrow. Is that all right with you? Roz, are you there?' Peter asked sharply when Roz didn't answer immediately.

Roz was thinking that everything was moving too fast for her. Barely back from one assignment, she was not sure she was ready to plunge into another one involving time abroad again. Nothing could ever be as shattering as the Zangyrian experience, but she needed breathing space... perhaps some unexciting local little job.

'Yes, yes, I can make it tomorrow.' Roz forced out some belated enthusiasm.

'Good. I told them two o'clock. You can change the time if it doesn't suit, but don't put them off, Roz.' Peter rang off.

If she'd told Peter she felt like skipping this job altogether, he'd have had her scalp, or struck her off his books—or both. Roz pulled herself together. She was not in the position yet of picking her own jobs, and she should thank her lucky stars that Lyn and Peter gave her any jobs at all, let alone the super ones they put her way.

Feeling more positive, Roz went out to do some long-overdue shopping for provisions. Then, on a complete whim, she walked into a salon and had her hair done.

For about eighteen months she had worn it pulled back into a ponytail, not particularly flattering and making her look rather severe—career-woman-like, Roz had told herself. Basically, she had worn her hair like that because she just didn't have the money to keep up visits to hair salons after she'd left James, and hadn't been much interested in the way she looked, anyway.

The reflection in the mirror when the trendy young man had finished with her, alarmed Roz;

it was so unlike her. Trimmed into layers and lightly permed for body, the hair fluffed around her face in a way her old-fashioned father would have termed as 'very fetching', but which made Roz feel a stranger to herself. And it must have been the stranger who walked out of the hair salon and trailed around innumerable dress shops and ended up buying two dresses. Roz could account for the first one—a comfortable shirt-waister in blue wool, ideal for the interview with the publisher, but there was no accounting for the second. The luxurious cream long-sleeved cashmere knit, that skimmed her body to her knees in a sensuous sweep, was an utter extravagance.

What on earth had she been thinking of? At the back of her mind had been the thought of the birthday visit to Cecily's, but Roz had remembered she wasn't going to go, then went on and bought the dress regardless. She returned home pleased with herself and the purchases, and quite looking forward to the meeting with the publisher and author the next day, until James telephoned shortly before she was due to set off to inform her he'd told Cecily they would both be coming on Sunday afternoon.

So much for his brief burst of caring and consideration—a one-day wonder! James was back in arrogant form, and Roz seized up with indignation, all her nervousness of him gone. This was the James she knew inside-out. On familiar ground, she launched into self-righteous attack. 'You had no right to do that. I hadn't said I'd come, I only said I'd think about it. And I have. The answer——' Roz wasn't quick enough to get the last word in before James interrupted.

'Cecily rang me, Rosalind—before I could get on to you to check what you'd decided. I didn't think you'd refuse—not for her birthday, so I told her we'd both be coming,' James explained with a carelessness that made Roz grind her teeth on the other end of the line.

'That's all very well, but——'

James cut her off again impatiently. 'All right, all right, so I jumped the gun. I'm sorry,' he conceded irritably. 'I'm frantically busy now, Rosalind, and haven't the time to argue with you. I'll pick you up at one-thirty on Sunday.' James hung up in her ear, leaving her riled and with the publisher's appointment less than an hour away.

CHAPTER FIVE

Roz stood in front of the long mirror in her bedroom, staring at her own reflection and wondering whether her subconscious had played a mean, underhand trick on her in getting her to buy the cream cashmere dress.

It was very lovely, and her eyes told her she looked great in it, especially with the new hairstyle, but they also told her that it was not Roz Davies the career woman looking back at her, but Mrs James Thornton. This was how James had loved her to dress—simply, elegantly. And ultimately femininely. What was she doing in it? And what was James going to think? That she had bought it for his benefit? That she was sending out signals that she was ready to take the first—backward—step into her former life?

He was due in ten minutes to pick her up for the birthday visit to Cecily. Roz had intended to call him back after her interview with the publisher and tell him there was no way she was going to come with him and he could tell Cecily any lie he liked to account for her absence. However, her intention had gone askew in the burst of wellbeing after hearing the details of the exciting new assignment, when she had felt so good about everything that she hadn't wanted to spoil the feeling by ringing James and putting on a tantrum to get out of the visit.

It was too late now to renege, but she could change into something else. Roz whirled to the wardrobe and pulled out the businesslike new blue dress just as the buzzer sounded. She stood with it in her hand for a moment, lips pursed, before tossing it across the bed. The cashmere it was to be, and let James think what he would!

Picking up her handbag and the bouquet of flowers she had bought for Cecily, Roz let herself out of the flat, opening the front door to James with a bad-tempered fling, and then was absurdly flattered as James's initial startled look slowly changed into one of open admiration as he took her in.

'You look lovely,' he said with his surprise still in his voice, and stood there looking for all the world like an overawed swain.

'Thank you,' Roz muttered, all at once self-conscious and flushing idiotically, feeling as if she was going out on a date with him.

'I like your hair like that, it's very... it suits you,' James changed the compliment mid-stream and Roz suspected that the word on the tip of his tongue had been something like 'feminine', only he'd thought better of using it.

'Thanks,' Roz muttered again. Then, catching the quizzical speculation behind the lingering smile in James's eyes, she added shrewishly as they went out the gate, 'Don't flatter yourself it's all for your benefit. I had to spruce myself up for the meeting I had with the publisher on Friday about my new assignment.' And that should put him in his place, thought Roz tartly. 'And furthermore,' she picked up the hectoring tone when she was settled in her seat and James was setting the Porsche smoothly into motion, 'I did not appreciate having this visit foisted on me with such deviousness.'

'I've already explained how that came about, Rosalind, and there wasn't any deviousness involved at all. I just didn't think you would want to let Cecily down. Let's not spoil the afternoon by bickering. Why don't you tell me about your new project?' James suggested, changing the subject without any attempt to be subtle about it.

Roz came off her high horse in spite of herself. The project was of the kind any photographer would kill for and, after Zangyria, seemed like something out of a fairy-tale—putting together a collection of photographs on the out-of-the-way street markets of Greece. And later, if the first book took off, there would be a series ... Italy, France and who knew what else? She was thrilled to bits and not so put out with James that she wasn't prepared to babble on at length about how wonderful it was all going to be and how much she was going to get out of this assignment, overdoing the gush a little but wanting James not to miss the point—that her post-Zangyrian hysteria and doubts had been no more than a temporary aberration and were behind her; she was her professional self again and raring to go. 'It's going to be such fun. Fun. I've almost forgotten the meaning of the word,' Roz fairly trilled.

'You and me both,' James muttered under his breath.

'I'll be going over there for a week or so with the author in two months' time, so he can show me what he's after...' Roz stole a sidelong glance through her lashes at James's profile, trying to gauge whether there was any reaction to her deliberate disclosure that the author was a man; there wasn't, and she was aware of a silly disappointment. 'He'll drive me around to the various places he has already picked out, and I'll take some preliminary shots. Then later, I'll go back alone for about a month to do the collection, but we need to be together initially so I'm quite clear about what he wants in the photographs.'

Carefully withholding the fact that the author was a weedy little chap, married, and taking along his wife and two kids for the ride, Roz laboured her point home and wondered why she bothered, why it mattered to her that James didn't seem particularly interested whether she went off with a Greek Adonis or a hen-pecked travel writer. Why should he be, when he probably assumed there were men in her life as a matter of course—just as she assumed there were women in his? That was what being sophisticated was all about, wasn't it?

'It's going to be more like a holiday than anything else,' Roz finished with forced gaiety, and got a rise out of James at last.

'Nice work, if you can get it. I wouldn't mind it myself,' he said with genuine envy.

'You should change your job, then,' Roz returned smugly. 'How is it going, by the way?'

'What?'

'*Your* job. How is the state of the newspaper empire?' she enquired flippantly.

James turned to her, and their eyes engaged briefly. 'Do you really want to know?'

Slightly nonplussed by the seriousness of James's tone, Roz gave a small laugh. 'No, thanks,' she replied dismissively. Since he had succeeded his late father to the chairmanship of the family's newspaper organisation, James had rarely talked about his work; Roz was not even sure what a chairman did—something unutterably stuffy, she presumed, like taking over newspapers.

The corner of James's mouth curled upwards in a bitter little twist as he returned his eyes to the road, and in that moment Roz felt a stab of shame for having been so uninterested and so mocking about such an important part of James's life. There had been something callous about her attitude, unthinking, but unpleasant none the less, especially after James had made an effort to at least seem interested in her work, much as he disliked it. And, when Roz came to think about it, her work, one way or another, had been the sole topic of conversation between them on virtually every occasion they'd met since she had got off that plane from Zangyria.

Her conscience pricking, Roz said contritely, 'I'm sorry, James. I didn't mean to sound so flippant. I'd like very much to hear what you've been doing.'

James kept his eyes fixed straight ahead. 'I wouldn't dream of boring you,' he said stiffly, and Roz flushed at the neatly administered snub—no more than she deserved, but it rankled.

After that, they fell into a terse silence which lasted until they took the turn-off from the motorway. When they were within sight of the village, James flicked her a glance and said, with as much expression as if he was telling her the time of day, 'I've told Cecily we're getting back together again, so I'd appreciate it if you played along and acted accordingly.'

Roz didn't do or say anything for a long moment; she was stunned out of her wits. She opened her mouth and shut it again; then, still stunned, swung around to James's grim profile. 'You what?'

'You heard.'

'Oh, I heard all right, I just don't believe it! You've got to be joking.' Nothing about James indicated a joke. Roz fell back in her seat. 'I don't believe it,' she repeated weakly. 'If that's your idea of a birthday present for your mother, you can count me out. I don't know what you think you're doing, let alone why, but I'm not going to be party to it, James. Not for you, not for Cecily.'

'It won't kill you, Rosalind. Cecily has been very unwell and . . .'

'Unwell? What do you mean, "unwell"?' Diverted momentarily from the main point, Roz reacted with alarm.

'She had pneumonia a couple of months ago—mild, but at her age it took a lot out of her.'

'Then why didn't you tell me? You should have told me,' Roz cried out, angry and shocked that James could have kept such a thing from her.

James suppressed what sounded like the start of an angry laugh. 'You weren't exactly receptive to any communications from me,' he pointed out with a bite.

It was true, she had made it virtually impossible for James to get in touch with her, but she would have made an exception where news of Cecily was concerned. Surely James would have known that. Or did he actually believe that she had become so self-absorbed, she wouldn't be able to find time for a sick old lady? It was a monstrous thought. Roz studied his stony profile in puzzlement, realising she had very little idea of what went on behind the hard, handsome façade of James's face any more. Had she ever?

'I'm not going to do it, James,' Roz said firmly as they drove in through the gates and into the parkland surrounding the Thornton family home. 'Cecily might be old and unwell, but she's not stupid and she wouldn't fall for the charade for a moment. And, even if she did, what happens when it's all over? Because I do still want the divorce, and nothing is going to change that.'

James refused to answer. They were already sweeping up the drive in front of the large

Georgian house. Letting out a grinding sound of exasperation, Roz reached to the back seat and lifted out the bouquet of flowers.

'Don't let me down, Rosalind,' James ordered as he opened the car door for her, and Roz read a vague threat into the words. 'For Cecily's sake,' he added pointedly. And, since Cecily Thornton was emerging through the front door at that very moment, Roz gave him a quick glare and hurried towards the old lady.

Giving her a warm hug and a kiss on the lined cheek, Roz thrust the flowers into her mother-in-law's hands. 'Happy birthday for tomorrow, Cecily, and I'm sorry it's been so long,' she mumbled contritely.

Cecily drew back a little and studied Roz's embarrassed face with a smile. 'It's so lovely to see you again, darling,' she said softly as James came up to them. He gave his mother a kiss, then put an arm—a very proprietorial arm—around Roz's shoulder. Pink with pleasure, Cecily looked from one to the other. 'Oh, my dears, I'm so pleased to see you!'

Together. See them together, that's what she meant, Roz thought angrily as James's arm tightened warningly around her shoulder.

They followed Cecily into the house and into one of the smaller reception rooms off the wide, gracious hall. The room overlooked the terrace which ran the full length of the house. 'We'll have tea in here. I've had a fire lit for cosiness, and because I must confess I do seem to feel the chill so much more these days. I'll just organise these beautiful flowers and see if Lucy has the tea ready. You two make yourselves at home.' Cecily beamed at them lovingly.

Roz flung off James's arm the moment they were alone. 'This is mad, James. Mad and cruel!' she hissed. 'I'm not going to stand by and have her think we're all lovey-dovey again. I'm going to tell her just how things really are between us.'

'You'll do no such thing, Rosalind. I forbid you.'

'Forbid?' The old-fashioned word jolted a laugh out of her.

'Yes, forbid,' James repeated stonily. 'Cecily has been looking forward to this afternoon, and I'm not going to let you spoil it for her with your version of grim reality. She's barely over the pneumonia, and worrying about you—about us,' he amended brusquely, 'hasn't helped. If you stopped being so selfish and thought of somebody other than yourself for a change, you'd see it wouldn't hurt you to play along for an afternoon and make a sick old lady happy.' James moved away from her as Cecily came back into the room.

Roz forced a hasty smile to her lips and took a surreptitiously careful look at her mother-in-law. On the surface, Cecily did not seem much changed: her grey hair was in its usual elegant knot at the nape; her eyes, their blueness faded a little, were still alert and kind; she had more lines, perhaps, but then one was entitled to a few more wrinkles at seventy. A lovely, gentle face. She did not look obviously ill, but the aftermath of her illness lay in the thinness which earlier had been an attractive slimness, and in the air of fragility that Roz couldn't remember being in evidence the last time she had seen her.

'Come along, come along.' Cecily shepherded them towards the sofas by the fireplace, where afternoon tea in the form of an assortment of sandwiches and cakes was already set up on a nearby trolley and only waiting for Lucy to appear with the tea.

Cecily had not lost her touch; under her skilful, subtle management, Roz's tension fell away by degrees as they talked pleasantly of village happenings, neighbouring families, about Roz's father. They even touched on Zangyria, which Roz found she could talk about without any of the emotion she had displayed to James only a few days earlier. And when, a little while later, James produced the small gift-wrapped box and presented it to his mother as being 'from both of us', Roz was relaxed enough to let the lie ride without protest.

The gift turned out to be a beautiful pearl brooch, and Cecily was delighted with it, pinning it on to her blue-grey dress immediately and thanking them both warmly. Roz let that ride, too, and aware James was watching her nervously she gave him a faintly conspiratorial smile, which might have been taken by Cecily as affectionately wifely. It was taken by James with relief; he smiled back at her quickly, and overall their charade must have appeared a great success. Roz felt a twinge of guilt at the trick they were playing on the old lady, and hoped James had the grace to feel rotten about it, too.

He had been very quiet, distracted rather, as if his mind was elsewhere—or perhaps it was just nervousness, Roz thought, unaccountably feeling less hostile towards him and smiling, genuinely this time, as their eyes met over the coffee-table.

Declining Cecily's offer of a second cup of tea, and leaving his cake half eaten, James suddenly sprang to his feet. 'I've a few things to see Matthew about,' he said, referring to the housekeeper's husband, who did duty as Cecily's chauffeur and butler when the need arose. 'You won't mind if I leave you for a while, will you?'

Cecily's eyes followed him fondly out of the room, then settled back on Roz.

'Cecily, I'm awfully sorry I didn't get in touch when you were ill,' Roz began in a rush, wanting to get her guilt off her chest. 'I didn't ... well, I ...' she trailed off lamely, a peculiar sense of loyalty to James preventing her from telling that James had kept Cecily's illness from her.

Cecily smiled gently. 'I wasn't so very ill, darling, and I know you didn't know because I asked James not to worry you with it.' The charming smile edged into wryness. 'So you don't have to try and cover for James or pretend anything any more, darling. You see, I rather suspect you two haven't yet resolved your differences, and are still at loggerheads, in spite of putting on such a lovely show for me today.'

Roz didn't know where to look. Blushing like a schoolgirl, she tried to stammer something.

'It's all right, Rosalind,' Cecily assured her, 'there's no need to feel embarrassed. It was a sweet idea—James's, I presume, since it was a little silly, and not the sort of thing you would think of.'

So much for James taking his mother for a naïve old thing! Cecily Thornton was as shrewd as they came. Roz grinned sheepishly.

'He meant well by his little deceit; he knows I've been taking your separation rather hard. Now, don't look like that, darling,' Cecily admonished mildly as Roz dropped her eyes guiltily and stared down at her cashmere-covered lap. 'I'm not blaming you—either of you. I thought I made that clear to you a long time ago. These things happen—need to happen sometimes. In a way, I think it's done you good. You've changed, you know, Rosalind.'

Roz glanced up.

'Yes, you have. I can sense it.' The old lady nodded pensively. 'You seem much more self-assured.'

'Well, perhaps I'm not quite the rabbit I used to be,' Roz conceded with an abrupt laugh, remembering how intimidated she had been by James's family when she'd first joined it. She had warmed to Cecily very soon, but Adrian Thornton, for all his attempts to put her at her ease, had rendered her almost speechless with awe and self-consciousness. There had been a positive horde of aged and very self-important aunts, too, with the odd uncle to match—mercifully rarely met, but never forgotten.

'You were never that,' Cecily chuckled. 'You were rather timid though, but I always felt you were a strong person underneath, and only needed to grow into your own strength.'

Strong? The very last word Roz would have chosen to apply to herself. If Cecily only guessed at half the doubts that kept Roz lying awake at night, lonely and scared, and wondering where she was heading.

'Stronger than James, in some ways,' Cecily said, astonishing Roz even more. 'He took your leaving very hard, you know. I was very worried about him, what with it coming so soon after all those business problems which he'd only just managed to sort out. It was a very bad time for him.'

What business problems? Roz checked the question as Cecily went on worriedly, her forehead a sea of wrinkles.

'And now they've started all over again, and I think James is under such strain that he's not thinking very clearly these days—trying to play games with his old mother, among other things.' Cecily smiled indulgently. 'And himself, too,' she added, her smile fading away into sadness. 'A case of wishful thinking going a little askew, I suppose. Still, one does need something to hold on to, and it's very difficult letting go of all the happy hopes and plans one had, isn't it?' She looked bleak, and very old all at once. 'My special hope was to be a grandmother before I died.'

Roz felt her face freezing over as she stared back glassy-eyed at her mother-in-law.

Cecily's expression underwent instant change, a vividly bright pink sweeping up her lined cheeks in a rapid wave. 'Forgive me, Rosalind, I don't know what got into me,' she said, appalled.

'James . . . I . . . we both decided against having children,' Roz mumbled, flustered. It was true in its way—if you ignored the fact that the decisions had never coincided.

Awash with embarrassment, Cecily got to her feet and came to put an awkward hand on Roz's shoulder. 'No, please, you don't owe me any explanations. I had no right to imply... Would you excuse me for a moment?' She left the room in agitated haste, and Roz jumped up too, and went over to the window. She was immeasurably upset by Cecily's comment, however unthinking it had been and, deep down, angry with the old lady. James and Cecily weren't the only ones to have had their 'happy hopes and plans' go up in smoke. Didn't anyone realise that Roz had her regrets, too? Where were the children she and James had talked about so happily during their engagement?

She had wanted to start a family immediately after they had got married, thinking James would want that too, but James had insisted they wait a while—possibly for Roz herself to grow up first, although he had never quite put it like that. It was only in their last six months together, when he began to spend more time at home, that James brought up the subject of children again, by which time it had been much too late: there had been eighteen angry, confused months in between when Roz had had to look for fulfilment elsewhere and, even if by default, had found it, establishing a whole new set of priorities for herself which no longer included James, let alone children. She had told him then that the claptrap about having babies to save defunct marriages had gone out with the Ark, and was very careful not to become pregnant—an academic precaution in the main, since they so rarely made love.

Perhaps things might have turned out differently if they'd had a child in their first, happy year together . . . grown into a family, instead of growing further and further apart, until the gap became unbridgeable and the only thing left was to go their separate ways, in spite of James's obstinate insistence, even now, that he wasn't prepared to give up on the marriage without a fight. But that was James being James—tunnel-visioned and wanting his own way to the last.

Roz's eye caught the figure of her husband walking, preoccupied, in the lengthening shadows of the garden at the foot of the terrace. He looked as vulnerable and lonely as she felt, and for an instant Roz experienced a searing regret for the life they might have had together. If things had been different . . .

On an inexplicable impulse, she opened the french window and slipped out on to the terrace, making a determined effort to shake off the depressing fit of nostalgia as she went down the steps to where James was, but something of her mood must have lingered.

James's eyes combed over her face searchingly. 'Is everything all right, Rosalind?'

'Yes, of course, why shouldn't it be?' Roz answered lightly. 'Unless you consider Cecily seeing through your little charade a major catastrophe.'

James made a groaning sound in his throat.

'Yes, she saw through it right from the start,' Roz told him cheerfully, and wondered again how James could have been so thick as to take his mother for an idiot. 'Mind you, she did think it was sweet of you, but a bit silly all the same. It was silly, you know.' She grinned at him without malice.

James grinned back ruefully. 'It sounded like a good idea at the time. What else did she say?' he asked, curious.

'Nothing much. We just talked a little about this and that.' Roz did not elaborate, and they started strolling along the path, going beyond the edge of the terrace and towards the bench in the shelter of the shrubbery behind it. When they reached it, they sat down, accidentally close, so that their arms were touching slightly. Roz remained where she was. And so did James.

'What has been going on at work, James?' she brought up the question as casually as possible. It had been preying on her mind since Cecily had mentioned those unnamed 'problems', and assumed Roz knew all about them.

'Why? What has Cecily been telling you?' James shot back in a suspicious growl.

'She hasn't been telling me anything,' Roz assured him hurriedly, taken aback by the unexpected hostility, but more perturbed than resentful. What was James so intent on keeping from her? 'Is it to do with that takeover you mentioned before?' She persisted with the longshot guess, and knew from James's face she was on the right track.

'You wouldn't be interested,' James muttered, turning away from her and staring ahead across the lawn which ran smoothly towards the ornamental lake.

Rebuffed, Roz stared at it, too. Why go on if James didn't want to talk about it? It was probably some temporary obstacle holding up the acquisition of some magazine or newspaper she'd never heard of, and James was right: she was not exactly agog with interest about the ins and outs of it, any more than she had been when he'd mentioned the takeover after she had burst in on his meeting last week. Yet Cecily was seriously worried, and Cecily was not the sort of person who made mountains out of molehills.

'I'm sorry if you thought I was prying. I wasn't. I was just...' Roz left the sentence hanging in the air. She was what? Concerned? The disconcerting answer to that was yes. She was concerned, not about any takeover, but about James himself.

She felt James's shoulder move in a jerky shrug against her arm. 'I'm having a spot of bother with the board about the latest offer,' he told her grudgingly, as if he resented having to tell her even that little bit. 'It will all sort itself out in the next week or two, so don't give it another thought. Cecily does tend to exaggerate things.' James gave a dry smile, and Roz did not believe him for an instant. Cecily had never been prone to exaggeration and James knew it. He glanced away evasively, then jumped up from the bench with too much heartiness. 'Come on, we'd better go back in. It's almost dark, and Cecily will be wondering what's happened to us.'

He was shutting her out, making it plain he did not want to discuss his 'spot of bother' with her. Oddly, it hurt, but she didn't know how to get past the invisible barrier between them—as tangible as a brick wall.

Roz got to her feet, her expression composed into a neutral mask. 'Well, I hope things work out the way you want them to,' she couldn't help saying.

'Do you?' There was faint surprise in James's voice, in his eyes too, as they ranged over her face for a moment. Then, with a quirk of his mouth that might or might not have been a smile, James said softly, 'You never know, perhaps they just might at that.'

Looking up from her embroidery, Cecily welcomed them with a smile as they came in through the french window, James's arm lightly around Roz's shoulder as he led her into the room. Cecily's smile lingered, while those shrewd blue eyes seemed to size them up in a long, speculative look. A knowing look, it struck Roz as being, but what could Cecily possibly think she knew? Nothing had happened outside in the garden, other than that Roz had taken a very small step in an unfamiliar direction and had tried to talk to James. And had got nowhere.

Cecily took it for granted they would be staying to dinner—very likely because James had already made the arrangement with her, Roz surmised, but without resentment. After one or two half-hearted protests she gave in gracefully, and then was glad they had stayed.

She had not realised how much she had missed something as ordinary and normal as a family Sunday. Sitting around the dinner-table with Cecily and James gave Roz the feeling of being part of something familiar and secure, far removed from the solitary person who invariably ate from a tray on her lap sitting in front of the television.

Too familiar. And she was too much part of it. After dinner, when they returned to the drawing-room for coffee and port, Roz began to feel on edge. She kept casting meaningful looks at James—wifely, non-verbal communication—only she must have been out of practice because, instead of taking the hint and saying they must be leaving, James merely smiled lazily and went on sipping his port, while Cecily chattered on gently about one thing and another. Like old times. It was as if they had all been drawn into the subtle cosy net, but it seemed to Roz she was the only one who sensed the danger that lay behind the contented façade.

That was all it was—a façade, an illusion. And it disturbed her that Cecily might start getting ideas into her head and want to repeat the family occasion in the near future. That would be asking to be hurt, because the moment she and James walked out the door the illusion would vanish into the night air and everything would be back to square one.

Or would it? Roz was conscious that a change had crept into her attitude towards James, a change that couldn't entirely be attributed to the suspension of hostilities for Cecily's sake, nor to the quiet charm of the evening. Odd thoughts kept straying into her mind, 'what if' kind of thoughts. What if she did agree to have a lunch or two with James? What if they did make an effort to talk through some of the things they still so obviously had bottled up? It couldn't do any harm to try to clear the air a little, be a little more friendly. Like this evening.

'I think it's time we started back, James.' Roz abandoned the wifely looks and resorted to plain speech.

'Yes.' James glanced at his watch. 'Heavens, I hadn't realised how late it is.'

'We really did stay too long; Cecily was looking very tired there in the end,' Roz said in the car, careful not to sound accusing.

'Yes, we did. I'm sorry about that, I should have kept an eye on the time,' James was quick to apologise. 'Thank you for coming,' he said, almost formally, as they drove out the gates and left the Thornton grounds behind them. 'I know Cecily was very happy to see you.'

'I'm glad I came,' replied Roz, stating no more than the truth. For all its unsettling moments, she did not regret the visit, and those unexpected, uncomfortable moments had not really had anything to do with Cecily anyway, nor perhaps even James, but were the result of her own emotional loose ends fraying all over the place, when she'd thought she had stitched them all up neatly and put them away in a box in her mind marked 'The Past'.

Roz gave in involuntary sigh in the semi-darkness of the car. The trouble was, the past kept intruding; here she was, driving home with the man who was still her husband, from a social visit to her mother-in-law, no less, when on the other hand she was pressing for a divorce from that self-same husband. How much more muddled could you be?

'What?' muttered James, suddenly swinging the car to the side of the road; not a moment too soon, it seemed, for the car simply died on them. James let out a long groan. 'You wouldn't believe it! Out of petrol.'

Roz burst out laughing. 'I *don't* believe it!' It smacked so much of an adolescent ploy, she couldn't take it seriously.

'I'm not joking, Rosalind,' James assured her dismally. 'I must have been driving on empty for the last stretch of the way up and didn't even notice. Damn it! We'll never get any petrol at this time of night on a Sunday.'

Cecily had said James wasn't thinking clearly of late, but to drive about without even remembering to glance at the dashboard? Just how much strain was that takeover business putting on him? 'Never mind,' Roz murmured accommodatingly. 'We've just passed the village. We can go to the pub and ring Cecily from there, and she can send Matthew with a can of petrol,' Roz said firmly, and felt slightly strange in taking the initiative.

'No good. He doesn't keep anything more than a couple of litres on hand. Anyway, I don't want to disturb Cecily. It's been a tiring day for her, and she'll be just about in bed by now.'

'Well then, we'll have to book into the pub for the night. It's either that or spending the night in the car,' Roz stated the obvious, aware of a certain smugness that she was taking this so reasonably instead of flying off the handle and threatening to stomp off to Cecily's or something equally pig-headed.

'Well, if you don't mind . . .' James sounded dubious.

'Oh, come on, James!' Roz urged with cheerful impatience, and got out of the car.

CHAPTER SIX

THERE were lights glowing from practically every window when they reached the pub, arm in arm. They must have presented a cosy picture as they came into the foyer, but it was no more than good sense as far as Roz was concerned, since her high heels were not designed for walking along road-sides in the dark.

The place was abuzz with voices, and there were so many elderly ladies in evidence, it was quite astonishing.

'Bingo night, do you think?' James murmured the amused aside into her ear as they made their way to the reception counter, where a harassed, middle-aged man appeared to be handing over every key he owned to a young uniformed chap who looked like a bus driver, and an extremely unhappy one, as he took the heap of keys and moved away with a mutter to be swallowed up by the elderly contingent.

'You look busy tonight,' James observed pleasantly when the landlord's attention finally focused on them in a slight daze.

He rolled his eyes exaggeratedly up at the ceiling at James's understatement. 'Lord preserve me! A broken-down coach, a battalion of pensioner ladies and a driver about to follow his coach's example and have a complete breakdown,

too. What can I do for you, now?' The brave
attempt to sound like a genial host fell short of
its mark.

'We're sorry to add to your troubles,' James
began soothingly, 'but our car ran out of petrol
just down the road, and my wife and I need a
room for the night. The name is Thornton. Mr
and Mrs.'

'Two,' Roz put in hastily as 'a room' hit home.

'You, too, eh?' The landlord mistook Roz's
meaning. 'I'd like to help, but...' He gazed at
them glumly, shaking his head for an absurdly
long moment before stopping suddenly, his face
screwing up tightly in what must have been intense concentration. 'Wait a moment, let me
think. Now, what if I put the coach driver into
one of our own private rooms, and gave you the
one I've assigned to him. Yes, that's what I can
do,' he beamed, delighted by his own ingenuity.
'The poor chap won't care where he beds down
tonight—he's past caring, the state he's in! Just
wait here a moment and I'll track him down and
grab his key back from him.'

'James, I don't think...' Roz started in a tight
undertone as the landlord vanished at an ungainly gallop.

'Let's just consider ourselves lucky to get a
room at all, Rosalind,' James interposed,
knowing exactly what she was going to protest
about.

'Here we are, then.' The landlord bustled back,
pink from his exertion. 'We won't bother with
signing-in tonight, if you don't mind. I'll take

you right up now. The wife is running about making tea for the old biddies to calm them down. You won't be needing anything, will you?' he asked in a voice that made it very plain he hoped they would not.

'Nothing at all, thank you,' James assured him, keeping a hand on Roz's elbow and avoiding looking at her as they followed the man up the stairs and along the corridor, where the bus driver was staggering along, a suitcase in each hand and bags tucked under both arms.

'I'll give you a hand with those in a moment,' the landlord tossed over his shoulder to the driver. He led them to a door at the end of the corridor, unlocked it and handed James the key as he shepherded them into the room. 'The bathroom is two doors down. It's marked, so you can't miss it, and now, if there's nothing else ...'

'We'll be fine, thank you. Don't let us keep you,' James said in a pleasant dismissal.

The bed was a big double one, with old-fashioned, curved, wooden bed-ends. After the first horrified glance, Roz had determinedly kept her eyes from straying anywhere near it while the landlord was in the room, but now that he was gone the appalling piece of furniture drew her eyes like a magnet. Roz jerked them away and found herself looking straight into James's eyes, watchfully alert in an otherwise impassive face.

'No, James ...' Roz kept her voice down, despite her nervousness, remembering that the rooms all around were occupied, and that old ladies were not necessarily deaf ones.

James said nothing.

Roz shook her head mutely and looked wildly around the room. Bed aside, the furniture consisted of an oversized wardrobe, a chunky chest of drawers with a mirror on top of it, and two uncomfortable-looking armchairs in shabby, blotched vinyl, circa early sixties. They had no armrests and pushed together... She glanced back at James. He gave a grimace of distaste as he got the message as to where he was supposed to sleep, but didn't voice any protest, just shrugged carelessly.

Faintly surprised that he was going to be so reasonable about the sleeping arrangements, Roz let out an audible sigh of relief. Catching it, James smiled drily, one dark eyebrow rising quizzically in an amused question.

Roz went red. She jerked her eyes away, feeling stupid, and annoyed with herself for having let James glimpse how panicky she had been.

'I'm going to go downstairs to see if our hapless host can be persuaded to rustle me up a drink. So why don't you use the bathroom before the old dears take over?' James suggested with a wry helpfulness, relieving her of the last of her worries. Then he left, closing the door softly behind him.

Roz sprang into action. Grabbing the towel from the end of the bed, she darted out of the room and into the bathroom, bolting in and out of the shower with lightning speed. Then, dampish and breathless, she scrambled into her petticoat again and, checking that the coast was clear, was back in the room almost in the time it would have taken James just to walk down the stairs! With a bit of luck, the landlord would be so grateful for some calm male company, he'd press James into several drinks, and she would be feigning sleep well before James returned.

Roz threw her clothes untidily into the wardrobe and hurriedly pushed the two armchairs together. Then, taking a blanket from the bed, she spread it over them, and as an afterthought she added one of the pillows. Standing back, she surveyed the makeshift bed critically. It looked horribly unenticing, and would probably be about as comfortable as the rack for a six-foot man, but that couldn't be helped and James would just have to lump it for one night.

About to jump into bed, Roz remembered the light and dashed across the room to the switch by the door. Her hand was raised, fingers an inch from the switch, when the door was flung open. James came into the room casually, but from the rise and fall of his chest he looked as if he had pelted up the stairs two at a time and finished with a sprint down the length of the corridor!

There was a moment of stock stillness as they stared at each other. Then, in a sort of slow-motion delayed action, Roz dropped her hand and took a step back. The wardrobe was too far away to make a snatch for her dress and, under the circumstances, it was a little late in the day, not to say stupid, to start playing the modest virgin. They were husband and wife; James had seen her in a petticoat before. He had seen her naked and, the way he was looking at this moment, she might as well have been.

'I thought you were going to stay downstairs,' Roz accused shakily.

James shut the door. 'I changed my mind,' he said coolly, as if the change was of no consequence whatsoever. Taking off his jacket, he tossed it over the back of one of the armchairs, appearing not to have noticed their new arrangement, or if he had, simply ignoring it.

'What are you doing?' Roz's voice rather squeaked the question. A stupid question.

'Getting undressed. What does it look like?' James countered lightly as he peeled off the cream sweater and dropped it on to the jacket, then continued to undress with the unhurried nonchalance of all those innumerable other times he had undressed in front of her.

Only this was not one of them, and Roz's heart started to pound nineteen to the dozen as she watched, unable to help herself, running her eyes across James's broad, muscled shoulders, over his chest and following the downward path of the dark hair which tapered into the hard flatness of his stomach, before wrenching them away and bringing them back to James's face. Her mouth was suddenly so dry, it hurt when she tried to swallow.

'Time's up, Rosalind, we're not going to pretend any more. I want to make love to you; you want to make love to me. Isn't that why we're here?'

James's voice was soft but almost matter of fact, telling her no more than she knew herself. But hearing it voiced sent a tremor of shock through her. Then, as James's mouth curved into a tantalising promise, Roz's mind went into a wild spin of erotic anticipation that made her feel dizzy.

This is madness, the fragment of her mind that was still capable of rational thought was screaming at her. What she wanted, what she was about to do, was crazy and she would live to regret it. Roz knew that as surely as she knew that every step since leaving the car had been leading to this moment. Mouthing protest and acting alarmed had been a matter of form, no more than the playing out of an absurd face-saving little game, and now, as James said, it was time to stop pretending—to herself.

She did want James to make love to her. She could tell herself anything she liked, but she was in this room for no other reason because, in spite of James's reluctance, she could have rung Cecily and gone back to stay with her, or even opted for spending the night in the car—uncomfortable, yet an alternative, had she genuinely wanted one.

Later, much, much later, Roz was to remember that it was she who had made the next move to close the short distance between them, going to James with her lips parted, her hands curving passionately around his head to bring his mouth down hard as her own pleaded for deeper, more urgent exploration. Reality wheeled hazily in and out of focus as Roz crushed herself against him, revelling mindlessly in the familiar pressure of his body against her. It had been so long . . . so long.

When James drew back, his heavy-lidded eyes glittered darkly at her—with triumph, Roz thought with a jolt. But his fingers fumbled with uncharacteristic clumsiness at the straps of her petticoat, and Roz felt his hands tremble as they slid the straps over her shoulders and peeled the soft, silky garment down her body.

'James, please . . .' Her nerves haywire, Roz begged raggedly for an end to the frustrating preamble, and for a split second felt a sting of humiliation that her physical need of him was robbing her of her last shred of pride.

James stepped back and looked at her as if this was the first time and he had never seen her body before. Roz felt nineteen again, on their wedding night—shy, terribly vulnerable and breathless with excitement. Then, she had been a little frightened of what was to follow; now, she was frightened of her own body, which was acting out of its own needs and way out of her control.

She started to shake uncontrollably, ice-cold with intense excitement, while her eyes pleaded mutely, and at last James swept her up in his arms and carried her to the bed.

She lay where he placed her, unnaturally still, and watched as James knelt on the bed beside her and looked at her again, his eyes exploring, lingering. Possessing. She wanted to touch him, to pull him down to her, yet felt compelled to offer herself to the exploration of those burning eyes for as long as James wanted.

Head swimming, Roz pressed her eyes shut, and when she opened them the light hurt. 'The light...' she murmured.

James was gazing into her face. He gave a faint shake of the head. 'I want to see you, Rosalind,' he breathed unevenly at her. He lowered himself beside her at last, but stayed propped up on an elbow, so that their bodies did not touch as he bent over her.

Roz smothered a cry at the first contact of his hand with her warm skin, but couldn't hold back the moans of satisfaction as James's hand began to stroke and caress expertly in a languid path down her body, brushing fleetingly without lingering, and leaving a feverish ache everywhere it touched. And during every moment the smouldering eyes stayed on her face, already possessing her, while James restrained his own passion, intent on inciting hers.

Roz cried out something on an indrawn gasp, arching in wave upon sensuous wave as James brought his mouth over a hardened nipple. She felt she was subsiding into a bottomless whirlpool of sheer, helpless pleasure, where nothing else existed but wonderful, mindless sensation. She heard herself making breathless, garbled sounds as she buried her lips into James's hair and dug her fingers fiercely into his shoulders; then, unable to bear it a moment longer, she frantically drew his head up to claim his mouth, all the time moving feverishly against him until

James was groaning hoarsely, caught up in their separate, yet mutual passion that was carrying them both to its inevitable peak.

James wrenched his head up, breathing in harsh gasps as his eyes burned down at her.

Roz gazed back at him through her lashes, her eyelids so heavy that she could barely keep them up. 'I want you, James. I want you,' she whispered passionately, and with the arm wrapped around his neck she tried to pull his mouth down to her again, every second of delay a torment.

'I know that, I've always known that,' James rasped impatiently. 'Now tell me that you love me,' he demanded.

Roz nodded wildly.

'Say it.'

'Yes, yes, yes! I love you.'

James gave a shuddering sigh, his face twisting into an agony of desire, and Roz cried out in a desperate delight as he entered her at last.

'I need you, darling, I need you.' She heard James's cry through the thudding in her ears before sound and time fused and stopped.

Roz awakened slowly. She kept surfacing to semi-consciousness and hazy awareness of the warm weight against her which felt familiar and which she sleepily knew was James; then, oddly comforted, she drifted back into light, easy sleep again until she woke properly. And remembered—everything, only couldn't believe it.

Her eyelids flicked open.

James was curled into her side, an arm over her hip, his face turned into her breast. In sleep, the lines of tension, which seemed to have grooved themselves into James's face of late, were relaxed, making him look softer and years younger, and so vulnerable that Roz felt momentarily uncomfortable to see him like that—with his defences down. It was like spying on someone through a keyhole.

Oh, God, Roz groaned inwardly. It was no use asking herself how last night had happened. There were a thousand and one excuses she could give herself, but only one touched the truth: last night happened because she had wanted it to happen. As much as James.

But what now?

Last night she had told James she loved him, when she had been so delirious with desire for him that she would have blurted out anything at all that he demanded, and then some. Yet, looking at him now, lying as trusting as a child beside her, Roz wasn't sure whether she could take it back. Not entirely. There was some disturbing feeling in her that went beyond straight-out physical attraction. Love? Or was it a sense of love past, the memory of something poignant and lovely which they had once shared, and which the visit to Cecily had brought out of the shadows of her subconscious?

James stirred against her, and instantly Roz held herself so still that she was actually holding her breath in an effort not to make any movement that might waken him and bring them face to face in the passionless clarity of the morning after. What were they going to say to one another when the moment could not be put off any longer? Carelessly shrug the episode off like two mature, sophisticated adults who had succumbed to their mutual attraction for each other?

Things like that happened all the time. They did—but not to her. To James, yes. Roz had few doubts on that score.

Was that how James would view their lovemaking—a score? Another woman to add to the tally of women seduced by his charm? Granted, it was his own estranged wife, but that would add a kind of perverse piquancy and an extra boost to his ego, because he had proved conclusively that she was still wildly attracted to him.

The thought that the night might have meant no more than scoring a point against her brought a dull pain to Roz's chest. Then how did she want James to feel—when she didn't know how she felt herself? That this was the beginning of some sort of reconciliation? He wanted that—or said he wanted it, and perhaps even did for his own obstinate reasons. James had cried out that he needed her—in his bed. Only one didn't spend one's life in bed, and Roz had long experience of the hard reality of their day-to-day life outside of the bedroom to remind her how little James had really needed her. Or she him in the end; she shouldn't forget that, Roz reminded herself sadly as her eyes traced the wisps of dark hair curling into James's neck. On impulse, she ran a finger lightly down one of the dark wisps and made herself uneasy by the tenderness of the small, sad little gesture. What on earth was going on inside her muddled head now? Roz didn't want to know.

Very gingerly, she began to ease herself away from James's sleeping form. Inch by tentative inch, she made it further to her side of the large bed, feeling James's hand sliding slackly off her body. When it dropped on to the bed, Roz froze, waiting to see whether the movement had jerked James awake, but he slept on as peacefully as the proverbial baby and, breathing a soft sigh of relief, she finally inched herself right out of the bed.

'What are you doing, Rosalind?'

Roz was standing with her back to the bed. She had just picked up her petticoat from the floor and was in the act of slipping it over her head. After the start in which her heart jumped into her mouth, Roz finished putting it on, outwardly calm except for her maddeningly trembling fingers. Then, moving to the wardrobe for the rest of her clothes, she said, still without looking at James, 'Getting dressed,' and almost added, what does it look like? but remembered that that was James's throwaway line.

'But the sun is barely up yet, Rosalind.' James protested. 'Come back to bed.'

She heard a hundred unspoken words, a dozen heart-stopping questions in that single request, and blocked her ears to every one of them. Her clothes in her arms, Roz looked to the bed, where James was sitting propped up against the bedhead. 'We might as well see if we can rustle

up some petrol and get an early start, don't you
think?'

She kept her voice bland and her eyes carefully
fixed above James's neck, and saw his smile turn
into a wince before his face took on the lines she
was so much more familiar with—hard, tense,
tight-lipped. It was as if he had suddenly slipped
on his daily mask and, oddly, it made Roz feel
safer—from herself. She could cope with a tense,
angry James, whereas in her emotionally mixed-
up state she couldn't trust her own feelings for
the vulnerable man she had seen sleeping at her
side. If that man were to spring out of the bed
now and take her in his arms and assure her it
had been something deeper than sexual need that
had driven them together, chances were she would
let herself believe him—and happily. It was for-
tunate James could not read her outlandish
thoughts. Or could he?

James contemplated her, frowning, as if he was
trying to work something out about her. Had she
given herself away already? Roz swung away
abruptly and walked to the door, opened it and
glanced up and down the corridor. There was no
one about and she pattered quickly out of the
room with the bundle of clothes and hurried to
the bathroom, too unnerved to finish dressing in
front of James. Stupid, given everything that had
occurred, but stupid might have been her middle
name this morning. And last night. And right
back to the moment she had accepted James's
lift at the airport. Looking back, that had been

the start of the trail of stupidities which had led in an unerring straight line to James's bed.

James had taken his cue and was up and dressed too when she returned.

'I've an electric shaver in the car. I'll shave before we set off,' he muttered, giving his chin a self-conscious rub as Roz's eyes glanced at the dark stubble.

The focus of her glance had been utterly inadvertent and she had not meant it as criticism—a wifely reproach? Roz gave a shrug to say he could do what he liked, went over to the chest of drawers and took her handbag from the top of it, then stiffened as she saw him coming up behind her in the mirror. Instinct warned her to bolt, but she didn't move, and the next moment it was too late because James slipped his hands around her, locking them at her waist. Roz went from stiff to absolutely rigid. Then, when James brought his face down into the curve of her shoulder, his mouth brushing aside the strands of hair to make contact with the bare skin of her neck, everything turned into chaos inside her, with pulses racing madly and nerve-ends flaring.

The arching of her neck to his lips was an involuntary reflex action that she could no more suppress than a sneeze. It was the go-ahead James was waiting for to bring his hands up from her waist and cup the soft, cashmere-enclosed mounds of her breasts.

Roz's crazy moment of response ended in a writhing panic as she made a vain attempt to twist herself free. 'Don't, James, please! Let me go.'

James lifted his face up and, after a moment, slid his hands down to her waist again, but didn't release her. Their eyes engaged in the mirror.

'Let me go, James,' Roz repeated in the sort of deadly calm voice people use to cover up the fact that they're anything but calm. Her gaze faltered, but she compelled herself to keep looking James steadily in the eye through sheer will-power.

'You can't keep up this act that nothing happened last night, Rosalind. We've got to talk,' James said with the edge of frustration in his voice.

'There's nothing to talk about.' What a pathetic lie, Roz thought as she said it. 'Let's just forget it. Now, please let me go.'

James's smile was a grimace. 'That's your solution to everything, isn't it? Forget it; ignore it; don't talk about it—lock it it away and stew about it.' James unclasped his hands from her waist and flung them up in the air in a gesture of defeat. Or disgust. 'All right, Rosalind,' he agreed angrily, 'if that's the way you want to play it...'

They went downstairs together, not talking, yet, their stony faces aside, probably not looking very different to an average couple who didn't radiate cheer and chatter at that time of the morning, either. The landlord's wife didn't seem to think there was anything odd about them when she came upon them at the foot of the stairs.

'Ah, Mr and Mrs Thornton, isn't it? My husband told me you turned up last night. I hope you've had a comfortable night,' she ran on blithely while Roz produced a bland little smile and held it tightly in place.

'I'm serving early breakfast of sorts in the dining room. Just tea and toast is all I can manage, I'm afraid. Some of the ladies are down already, so if you'd like to join them...' The woman swept a hand vaguely in the direction of the room off the reception area and bustled away with a distracted smile aimed nowhere in particular.

'Why don't you have something to eat while I try to raise someone at the garage? I'll come back for you when the car is ready to go,' James suggested with strained politeness.

'Yes, all right,' agreed Roz, reproducing his tone, and defied anyone listening to them to guess what had gone on between them five minutes earlier.

She spent half an hour drinking two cups of tea and idly toying with a piece of toast amid the twittering of excited old ladies who, if anything, appeared to find the breakdown of their coach even more thrilling this morning than they had the previous night. Hearing them rehashing the mishap, Roz had to conclude it ran pretty close to being the highlight of the trip to... wherever, and found herself envying them the simplicity of their uneventful lives. Not a man in sight between them, and probably not the least missed— a feminist's nirvana she was never going to reach with all her confusions and interminable doubts and disturbing regrets—the legacy of having been involved with a man like James Thornton.

Having been involved, or involved, present tense? Roz couldn't distinguish any more, her emotions were too off-course to enable her to think straight, and she was not sure she wanted to for fear of learning something she was better off not knowing. And was that a cop-out or emotional self-defence?

Roz sighed wearily as she stared down at her empty cup. She should have taken the opportunity upstairs to tell James their night of love-making had been nothing more than a casual fling for old times' sake, and put an end to it there and then; but she hadn't, and if she tried to do it now it would sound suspiciously as if the lady was protesting too much. And lying through her teeth!

Later, in the car, James made no attempt to talk. About anything. He had run the shaver over most of his stubble before collecting her from the reception area, but had made a hurried—or distracted—job of it and missed the odd patch, which must have been annoying him because he kept rubbing at them intermittently as they drove along, with only the monotonous low growl of the engine to take the edge off the thudding silence that was shredding Roz's nerves to pieces.

She couldn't even begin to think rationally with James sitting there beside her, his silent anger blasting at her like a blow-torch, while his oppressive closeness in the small sports car was sending her mind off along dreadful tracks. Snatches of the previous night kept flashing torridly in and out like some disjointed promotional clips for a blue movie. Roz was appalled with herself. She was going mad with the strain, and if this was playing it her way, it had certainly backfired on her; she hated every moment of it.

They hit the build-up of Monday morning traffic as they neared London. It grew more abominable with each mile, lengthening the trip unbearably, and by the time James swung the Porsche into the kerb outside her flat Roz felt she had been trapped for a lifetime. Her hand went flying to the door-handle. 'Thanks for the lift,' she sang out brightly, this side of hysteria by a hair's breadth, and scrambled out without giving James the chance to get in anything more than an urgent 'Rosalind!'

CHAPTER SEVEN

Roz changed out of the cashmere into her regulation navy slacks and cotton print shirt, and looked, if not felt, more like the self she was used to. She flung a jacket over her arm and was out of the flat and heading for the station within half an hour of James dropping her off.

'Oh, it's you. I wish you'd telephoned before you set off.' Lyn opened the cottage door to her with a wail and a bevy of cats curling around her ankles. 'I've been trying to get hold of you.'

'And *voilà*, your prayers are answered. Here I am,' Roz tossed back cheerfully, not the least put out by Lyn's peevish greeting. 'What did you want to talk to me about? The famine relief photos, I suppose.' She followed Lyn inside and into the kitchen and, taking off her jacket, looked vaguely about for a place to put it where the navy wool wouldn't instantly become a target for arching feline backs to rub against. She chose the door-knob.

'No. Yes. I mean, I did want to talk to you about the photos too, but Peter has just come up with a small local job he thought you might be interested in doing before you begin the Greek travel book. A catalogue for an antiques auction—nothing exciting, but something to fill in time. A little bit of money in it, too, of course,'

Lyn put in on an afterthought, uncharacteristically remembering that some people—like Roz—had a necessary interest in such mundane things. 'We want you to update your portfolio, that's what I was trying to get on to you about. You could have brought it over with you. Never mind, you'll be able to get it together for us in the next day or two, won't you?'

'Yes, I'll be glad to,' Roz assured her with a warm smile. Lyn was in wonderful, predictable form. No 'How are you, Roz, how are things?' just straight into what Lyn considered important: work. Roz could have laughed with relief. That was why she had come. If she'd stayed in the flat, she would have mooched about, driving herself up the wall. Lyn was exactly what she wanted at this moment to give her a totally different perspective on what mattered in her life: work; career. Personal dramas and traumas rated a very poor second with Lyn, and Roz urgently needed a little of that single-mindedness to rub off on her to put James back in his place.

'Coffee?' Lyn offered. 'Proper stuff. I remembered to buy in some beans at long last,' she added, pleased with herself for the housewifely aberration.

'Sounds delicious; yes, please. Any biscuits around?' Roz realised she was ravenous and gratefully polished off the inevitable crumbling crackers and aged chunks of cheese Lyn put out, without noticing what she was eating. 'Thanks, that was great,' she said when she finished. 'I was a mite peckish, wasn't I?' Roz smiled ruefully, then frowned, perplexed, as Lyn stood leaning back against the sink, the percolator in her hand and her head cocked to one side like an inquisitive sparrow studying a curious new breed of worm.

Roz ran a hand nervously through her hair.

'That's it! Got it!' Lyn announced triumphantly. 'It's your hair. I couldn't work out what was different about you, but it is your hair, isn't it? You've had it cut and curled...or something.'

'Or something,' Roz muttered waspishly, holding up her mug to be topped up, and feeling absurdly self-conscious that Lyn had noticed the new hair-style which she had forgotten all about.

'It's a bit like you used to wear it when you first started coming to photography class...pretty.' Lyn always made the word sound like a disease. Her own coiffure always looked as if it owed much to the pudding basin, and anything more than a self-administered snip at the fringe, in the interests of vision, was a waste of time in Lyn's book. Roz rather suspected Peter did the honours on the back of Lyn's head, working on the principle that what Lyn couldn't see couldn't bother her.

'So what's it in aid of?' Curiosity danced out of Lyn's cat-like green eyes.

'For heaven's sake, Lyn, there's no need to make an issue out of it! It's not in aid of anything,' Roz snapped in exasperation. 'I looked a mess when I came back from Zangyria and, since I had that meeting with the travel book publisher to go to last week, it seemed like a reasonable thing to spruce myself up for the occasion,' she explained—over-explained, testily, giving the same account of the strange whim she had given to James.

'Oh, yes...' Lyn didn't sound particularly convinced. 'I thought perhaps...' she began and thought better of it.

Roz had a pretty good idea what Lyn thought, and did not need three guesses to know her friend assumed James was somewhere behind the transformation—that Roz had tarted herself up to impress him, or something equally inane. It was just as well she was not still in the cashmere dress, or Lyn's wild imagination would really have been working overtime.

'Seen anything more of that husband of yours?' Lyn asked with a careless casualness that immediately confirmed Roz's suspicions as to the track Lyn's inquisitive mind had been speeding along.

She looked her blandly in the eye and ignored the question. 'Don't you think we ought to head to the studio and begin going through the Zangyrian stuff? I'm sorry I wasn't up to it the other day, but I'm fine now and that's why I came over here today.' Not entirely the truth, but as near enough as not to matter, and it worked.

'Yes, right.' James instantly banished, Lyn sprang up from straddling a chair and stepped on a cat. 'Sorry, sweetie.' She gave the aggrieved animal a quick pat. 'Leave those things there, Roz, we'll clean up later. Let's get to work now. I've already picked out what I think are the best

prints, but you can change them if you want. The
Relief Agency's publicity chap wants to have the
final say-so on Wednesday and then cart them
away the next day to set them up for Saturday,
so it's good that you've turned up today because
we haven't much time left. Anyway, they're
starting to clutter up the studio, and I want them
out of the way to make room for the other things
I'm working on.' Lyn's enthusiasm for a project
was in proportion to its novelty, and nothing was
as stale as the last assignment. Zangyria had just
about reached the end of its line as far as Lyn
was concerned—and Roz, too, for very different
reasons.

Roz became more and more absorbed as she
and Lyn sorted through the enormous collection
of photographs, discussing, arguing, comparing
the merits of one over another as they went along.
It was the antidote Roz needed to push everything else—and everybody from her mind—
James, Lyn's innuendoes, and her own confusions—an encouraging, hopeful indication that
her life did not, need not, revolve around James
and that, in spite of everything, her career was
as important to her as ever. Satisfied at last, Lyn
called it a day and they left the studio and went
back into the cottage.

And it was like breaking a spell and letting
reality in: a boring long train trip to an empty
flat and her own dismal company, with nothing
between her and the inevitable thoughts of James
but some vacuous television programme; a dis-
piriting prospect if ever there was one.

Tempted for a moment to ask Lyn to let her stay the night, Roz changed her mind, remembering with relief that Lyn wanted an updated portfolio and she could start working on that the minute she got home. If one collection of photographs could take her mind off things she didn't want to face, then surely so could another. And tomorrow would be another day. She would see Peter about the catalogue job, and the day after Lyn had arranged a meeting with the Relief Agency's publicity chap. Then there would be the final details of the fund-raising exhibition, and after that... Before she knew it, she would be back on even keel, and if James did happen to get in touch again she'd be calm and cool and distant, and very much the competent career woman, not the silly mixed-up little girl who didn't know her own mind.

Lyn had set about feeding the insistently miaowing cats which had trailed in from every corner of the house to gather expectantly in the kitchen. Roz counted seven of them and wondered how Lyn could stand them.

'No wonder they're starving, it's ages past their dinner, poor pets,' Lyn said sympathetically of the most well fed pack of felines Roz had ever seen. 'Speaking of which, Roz, have you any plans for this evening? Good,' Lyn smiled, pleased, as Roz returned a shake of the head. 'We've been working like slaves and deserve something for our efforts, so what say I ring Peter and tell him to pick up Michael—you know Michael Simmonds, don't you? No? Well, you'll like him anyway, and we'll all go out to dinner some-where. What do you think? Good idea?'

Roz looked at her indecisively.

'Now don't say "no", Roz,' Lyn got in before Roz could speak. 'You look as if you could do with a night out, if you don't mind my saying so. Don't worry,' she assured her lightly, 'I'm not about to pry into what, or who, is behind that edginess of yours. You worked like someone possessed back there in the studio, and I only hope you've managed to work it out of your system, whatever it was. Not that I couldn't hazard a guess. I'm not thick, you know.' Lyn grinned at her disarmingly.

Roz grinned back. 'I never said you were.' She only fell into the trap of thinking it from time to time, and usually regretted it. Lyn was as sharp as the proverbial tack. 'All right, I'll come,' Roz agreed suddenly, and rather surprised Lyn by giving in so readily. Why not? A night on the town sounded like a great idea: a drink—or three—and some uncomplicatedly pleasant company winning hands down over hours of solitary work and staring at the television.

They met up with Peter and his friend Michael at a new bistro Peter had recently 'discovered', but he had apparently kept his discovery to himself. The place was about three-quarters empty and the staff projected the rather des-perate *bonhomie* that makes you embarrassed for them, and only reinforces the faint bleakness of the surroundings. It was not quite what Roz had had in mind for a night on the town, having envisioned something bright and brash and so loud she wouldn't hear herself think.

And, to make matters worse, the minute introductions were over, she found herself paired off with Michael for pre-dinner drinks, so blatantly that it was embarrassing. A set-up no one could miss at fifty paces—in the dark at that. Lyn's doing, and possibly her spur-of-the-moment notion of doing Roz a favour. It smacked of Lyn putting two and two together and coming up with her standard five—get one man out of mind with another, and she could not have picked a worse way if she'd sat and thought about it for a week because, after James, Roz wanted nothing to do with men ever again.

Furious, Roz looked daggers at Lyn, trying to catch her eye to bring her and Peter back into more general conversation, and then had to give up before she went cross-eyed with the effort. Lyn simply ignored her, making a great show of hanging on Peter's every uninspiring word. Roz could have throttled her. Right, she thought snakily, and returned her attention to Michael, who hadn't left off talking for a second.

He was a pleasant enough young man, about her own age, and quite attractive in a wholesome sort of way, with his fair curly hair and even white teeth that shone at her in the flashes of nervous smiles. Her intention had been to freeze him off, but the intention faltered as Roz realised the poor chap was quite struck by her. Amused, she favoured him with a wide, super-brilliant smile and watched him actually blush, while his rate

of speech speeded up so much she would have
had difficulty making out what he was saying if
he hadn't repeated himself so often. It was all
about her; he had seen some of her work and was
determined to tell her at great length and very
earnestly how much he admired it. In spite of
herself, Roz was pleased by his innocent flattery,
and by the nervous sexual interest shining out so
incongruously from those baby-blue eyes.

Another time, she would have left it there, but
this was not another time; this was now, when
she had already drunk too much and was too
meanly enjoying herself to think sensibly of what
she was doing. It was fun encouraging Michael
for all she was worth, becoming more and more
outrageously flirtatious with every glass of wine,
until he must have been thinking all his Christ-
mases were about to come at once, responding
helplessly to her eye-batting charm throughout
dinner and gratifying Roz's ego no end.

Afterwards, in the loo, Lyn eyed her like a dis-
pleased headmistress. 'What are you trying to do
to him, Roz? For heaven's sake, go easy! He's
only a kid.'

'I don't know what you're talking about! I'm
having a lovely time. And, anyway, it was your
idea, so don't start coming over prim with me,'
Roz returned with a sulky snap, but she did feel
a momentary prick of conscience. What was she
trying to do? Make a fool of the young chap just
because she had made a fool of herself with
James? She didn't like the picture of herself using
someone so meanly and she shrugged it off.

'Michael is taking me home in a cab, so I shan't need to trouble you for a lift,' Roz told Lyn loftily.

Later, she was very sorry she had agreed to such a silly arrangement, when Michael insisted on holding her hand all the way to the flat, and even sorrier when, keeping the cab waiting, he took her to the door and asked when—when, not if—he could see her again.

Having given him a shameless come-on all evening, Roz started to back off in a hurry. 'I'm afraid I'm awfully busy at the moment. I've so many things on that I honestly can't say when I'll have a moment free, but why don't you try giving me a call in a couple of weeks?' she felt obliged to add, trusting that, by then, her *femme-fatale* attraction would have worn off and, with a bit of luck, he would have forgotten all about her.

Michael's face fell. The visible disappointment was almost childlike in its openness, but lasted only briefly before his face tensed into a recognition of her brush-off. He was too nice or simply too inexperienced to start putting any pressure on her after that. Roz felt a heel and, out of guilt, and because she thought him nice, let him claim his goodnight kiss.

They broke apart hastily as the gate gave an earth-shattering slam and turned to see James take the short path in about three furious strides. With the streetlight at his back his face was in shadow, but that made him look even more threatening. Jumping to the quite reasonable conclusion that James was some sort of intruder bent on no good, Michael flung a protective arm around Roz's shoulder, pulling her tightly against himself. 'What the hell do you want?' he demanded with a fierceness that surprised Roz.

'And what the hell are *you* doing with my wife?' James barked back, and, taking a step towards Michael, looked ready to pluck him off the doorstep.

Michael jerked an amazed glance at Roz's frozen face and must have seen in it all he needed to know. The next moment, his hand came flying off her shoulder. 'I . . . your . . .'

'That's right. My wife.' James grabbed hold of him and propelled him down the path with a shove. 'Your cab is waiting. No need to say goodnight, we'll take it as said,' he called after him with vicious sarcasm as Michael fairly bolted out the gate without a backward glance.

'How dare you? How *dare* you?' Roz could barely speak for fury.

James's fingers sank into her forearm as if he was expecting her to follow Michael down the path. 'Give me your key.'

'If you think you're coming in . . .'

'Key,' James snapped savagely.

Roz glared at him in helpless anger, wanting to defy him and tell him to go to hell. But they had made so much racket already that, in another moment, the upstairs tenant would be putting her head out of the window and telling them to shut up—or calling the police. Hands shaking, Roz fumbled in her handbag and produced her keyring.

James snatched it out of her hand and, unlocking the door, pushed her into the hall. Then, still gripping her arm, he unlocked the door to her flat and pushed her into that, too. Roz flicked on the light and stormed ahead down the corridor to get them away from the door and the hall, that was like an echo chamber at this time of night, carrying every sound up the stairs into the neighbour's flat. James followed, literally breathing down her neck.

Three steps into the sitting-room she spun around hands on hips and faced him. 'Right,' she grated out tightly, restraining the violent urge to yell at him. 'You'd better have a damned good explanation for forcing your way in here at one o'clock in the morning!'

James remained in the doorway, scowling at her. 'I've been waiting for you since six o'clock,' he accused peevishly, and looked as if he had, too, with everything about him looking worn out. He had obviously gone home to change into the business suit before going into the office that morning, but the suit and shirt both told of long hours scrunched up in the car, and Roz was a little shocked that he had put himself through such a mill to see her. But she was still too angry at his turn on the doorstep to make any allowance.

'I'm sure I don't know why you bothered,' she said icily, 'but I suggest you don't try it again, because if I ever find you lurking about like a peeping Tom, then threatening my friends, I'll call the police. I mean it, James.'

James moved edgily into the room. 'I was not lurking, and anyway, your little boyfriend looked as if he shouldn't be out alone. Where did you pick him up from—the local crèche?'

The sneer did not deserve a rejoinder. Roz contemplated her husband with contempt, and a dull satisfaction that his jealousy was showing; and somewhere in her subconscious she knew she was going to make use of it. She kept up the unblinking, disdainful gaze until James colored in an ugly wash of dark red.

'I'm sorry,' he muttered, giving a combined grimace and shake of the head. 'I didn't spend half the night waiting to see you just to annoy you.'

Roz stared and said nothing, and after a moment James began to pace restlessly around the room—working up to introducing the pub episode, Roz supposed. She was determined to make it as hard as she could for him. She did not want to talk about it. Now or ever, and a barricade of silence was her best defence.

James stopped his pacing in front of the bookcase and stood with his back to her, and Roz sat down at the table and studied the back impassively. Backs gave a lot away—as much as faces, and often more. You couldn't arrange a mask over the droop of the shoulders, nor disguise the air of weariness that hung over them like a cloak. James was dead on his feet, but it wasn't half a dozen hours of sitting in a car that was responsible for that. He was driving himself too hard. And for what? To add yet another paper to Allied Press's stables? The small glimmer of sympathy that had edged itself into her thoughts vanished.

Roz said coldly, 'This is ridiculous, James! I'm tired and I want you to leave. And don't come spying on me again.' He had not been spying, and the last bit was a deliberate nudge at his jealousy. Uncalled for and silly, but irresistible.

James turned to her slowly, his mouth a mocking twist. 'What, and miss your future heart-warming clinches with over-grown schoolboys? But, my prurience aside, Rosalind, you seem to forget I have a right to an interest in your affairs, since you still happen to be my wife.'

'That can very easily be changed,' Roz countered, sweetly, feeling she had the upper hand so long as she could manipulate James's jealousy.

'Don't count on it!' James jangled out a humourless laugh and turning sideways, suddenly spotted the tray, with a bottle each of whisky and sherry, that Roz kept on the small side-table that held the telephone. Without asking permission, he went over to it, picked up the whisky and carried it out to the kitchen, coming back with a half-filled glass and a bag of potato crisps that had been lying on the top of the bench. As Roz watched, he began to wolf them ravenously, taking quick gulps of the whisky in between large handfuls of the crisps he practically shovelled into his mouth. From the look of it, James might not have eaten all day, and it occurred to her that it was quite likely his last meal had been dinner at

Cecily's yesterday. His problem, not hers, if he couldn't take time out from his business hassles to feed himself, she thought, annoyed and uncomfortable at the sight of such unselfconscious hunger. Then she experienced a pang of guilt, remembering that James had taken time out from those same hassles to badger her into a meal when he'd thought she needed one.

James drained the glass and put it on the nearest flat surface, which happened to be an empty space between some books in the bookcase. He scrunched up the crisp bag and stuck it in there too, before turning to face her. Roz tensed. There was a perceptible change in James's movements—more purposeful, brisker, as if the hasty, impromptu meal of crisps and whisky had given him a charge of energy.

'I didn't sit for seven hours in the car, waiting for you to come home, to bandy insults or keep you from your sleep.' James spoke in a voice that had changed too, a no-nonsense voice that made Roz too nervous to think of trying any glib rejoinders. 'I know it's late, and I'm tired too, but I'm not leaving until we've thrashed out where we stand after last night—Sunday night—once and for all, because every moment we delay it, we make it more difficult for ourselves, and our futures are too important to play around with. I should have forced you into talking this morning, instead of letting you carry on with that rubbish of pretending nothing had happened. I made a bad mistake there,' James admitted, with a grimace that might have been intended for a self-derogatory smile.

Roz kept her eyes on him without wavering, and tried not to show how very frightened she was, waiting for him to get to the bottom line.

'Under the circumstances, it was a reasonable mistake, I suppose,' James went on. 'You were so uptight that I was too scared to open my mouth for fear of putting my foot in it. It might have had you backing off for good, digging in and pretending our night together hadn't meant a thing because you were too proud and too stubborn to admit you regretted leaving me, and, more to the point, that you still love me and want to come back to me. All the signs point to that, Rosalind, and I know you too well not to be able to read them.'

Up to that point, Roz had listened, her face rigidly set into showing nothing and belying the fact that James's words were getting through. He was not telling her anything she couldn't have worked out for herself if she had allowed herself to face where her behaviour and feelings were leading—had led to—and there was a moment approximating pure relief to hear it said aloud, and so rationally. But what her next thought or action might have been, Roz never knew, because it was then that James made the mistake of smiling—the soft, wry, almost teasing smile of the understanding husband being indulgent with his little wife who was too scatty to know what she was doing or what she wanted. That was how Roz saw it, and saw red.

Pushing back her chair with a jarring scrape, she was on her feet in a whirl of heated, unfocused hostility. 'That's exactly the sort of macho crap I would have expected from you!' she spat out like an affronted cat, eyes blazing and fur on end. 'One night in bed and I'm supposed to want to come crawling back to you.' Roz paused and gathered her next words for maximum impact—maximum hurt was what she was after. 'Well, I have news for you, James Thornton. What our night in bed meant to me was the same it meant to you—sex. S—E—X, sex,' she spelt out for him in sneering capital letters, and experienced a flare of triumph as she saw the disbelief and shock chase each other across James's face. She felt the corners of her mouth jerking upwards, but couldn't associate it with a smile. 'Oh, I thoroughly enjoyed it. You were always an excellent lover, James, I'll say that much for you, and you'll no doubt be pleased to know you still have the edge on most of the lovers I've had since I left you.' The travesty of a smile stayed in place, while inside Roz felt about to splinter into a million pieces. What was she saying? Why was she saying it? It was insane and it wasn't true, yet the need to hurt James was violent and overwhelming.

She savoured James's appalled face for a long moment, and then went on, because wild horses could not have stopped her. 'It's very obvious we still fancy each other and are great in bed together, and it might be rather pleasant to get together every now and then for another roll in the hay when we're not too busy.' It was as crude as Roz could allow herself to be, and she was amazed she wasn't physically sick saying it. 'But don't go getting ideas into your head, James,' she admonished playfully. 'I very definitely do not want to come back to you. My days of being a faithful little wife are long gone, and I do have other men interested in me these days, as you saw for yourself tonight.' Roz tried out a laugh and heard the ring of hysteria in it. She shut her mouth quickly and stared at him defiantly.

'I can't believe you, Rosalind!' James breathed out in hoarse shock.

'Try,' Roz suggested with grotesque flippancy, and thought James was going to hit her. She hoped he would—to knock the mad, spiteful cruelty out of her.

He was in front of her in one stride and seemingly in the same movement, cupping his hands around her face and yanking it towards himself so savagely that Roz's head felt as if it was being wrenched from her neck, and her ears sang with pain.

James's mouth forced her lips open without preamble to take his furious kiss, a kiss in name only; in deed, it was nothing more than an act of punishment and revenge, more violent than any actual assault could possibly have been. Roz's mind went into a momentary blank before her wits took over and she tried to drag herself away from him. When she couldn't get her mouth free, she began to hit agitatedly at James's chest. The attempt at struggle was futile, resulting only in inflaming James's anger. He pressed himself harder against her, bruising and hurting as he maneuvred her against the wall without unlocking his mouth from hers for a moment. Roz's lips had been rammed into numbness, and the brutally probing tongue in her mouth was tearing the breath out of her.

She had no idea when she began to return his furious passion, but she knew she had; her mind registered James's low growl of satisfaction at her mindless capitulation as he took his hands away from her head and, pushing open her jacket, deftly unbuttoned the top couple of buttons of her shirt with one hand before inserting them down the lacy curve of her petticoat.

Arching response, her body succumbed to the pleasurable sensation of the familiar touch, but her mind clamoured protest; this was not lovemaking and she was degrading herself every second she allowed herself to be manipulated like this . . . like some erotic mechanical doll. Roz tore her mouth away and stared, horrified, into James's face, where all the malice in the world glowed back at her from the glittering dark blue eyes. James's hand stayed inside her petticoat.

'No, James,' she pleaded in a distraught whisper, picking ineffectually at the hand on her breast.

James's laugh held mocking enjoyment. 'Why not, Rosalind, when you've only just told me how much you enjoy my lovemaking? And you're right; we are good together, so how about it?' he taunted, showing his teeth in a snarling parody of a smile.

Roz shook her head, then closed her eyes in mute humiliation and stood passively as James brought his mouth to hers again and teased at her clamped lips without any real attempt to force them open. He drew back after a moment or two.

'What's the matter, Rosalind? Don't tell me you're going to draw the line at making love to two men in one evening?' he asked in a show of spurious, spiteful interest. 'I would have thought you enjoyed sex far too much to be bothered by such unsophisticated scruples.'

The crude insinuation rushed the colour out of her face in a dizzying sweep and made her heart give such a lurch of shock that James must have felt the thump under the hand that lay over her breast. The next second, Roz's own hand landed on his cheek in a vicious, stinging slap that caught him off guard with that hateful, taunting smile still on his face. The room rang with the sound of the impact, and she would have slapped him again if James hadn't snatched his hand out of her blouse and, using both hands, grabbed hold of her wrists and nailed them down hard against her sides.

Roz watched the imprint of her palm come up on his cheek in a surge of mottled dark red. James's eyes held murder. 'Try that again and I'll slap you back so hard your teeth will rattle!' he rasped at her, his face so close that his breath scorched her cheek. 'And, if you think I insulted you, then I suggest you think again. You made it only too clear what it is you're offering, so stop acting like an affronted goody two-shoes when I take you up on your enticing little offer—along with the rest of your stable of studs.'

Roz couldn't believe what she was hearing. She gaped at him in stupid disbelief, her hands shaking from shock in James's numbing grip.

'Oh, yes!' James made a mechanical laughing sound, tightening his fingers around her wrists. 'You're twitching to slap me again for that, aren't you? But I swear it, Rosalind, I'll slap you right back—and enjoy it. Believe me, I'd like nothing better than to give you the hiding of your life, so don't tempt me.' James suddenly unclasped his fingers from her wrists and remained standing in front of her, his eyes daring her to take another swipe at him.

Roz was too shattered to even think of it. James had made out she was a tramp—or rather, her own wild attempt to show him how liberated and sophisticated she was had backfired grotesquely, and it was she herself who had made herself out to be the tramp. Roz felt so mortified that she couldn't look at him. She kept her eyes averted, desperately wanting to cry, and hating him for somehow bringing all this about.

Then James moved away from her at last, and Roz took two dazed steps to the chair and sank down on to it before her knees gave way and she fell over. Only a tiny core of pride prevented her from throwing her head on to the table and howling her eyes out. She stared hard through the open doorway into the corridor, not seeing a thing.

James was saying something. His words were a blur, but the sound of them broke through the blankness in her head and she turned to him expressionlessly.

'Did you hear what I said, Rosalind?' James asked sharply, and seemed to want some reaction from her, so Roz shook her head. 'I said you can have your divorce,' James said, almost carelessly, and waited, watching her face.

Roz didn't have a clue what it showed. She felt mildly bewildered that James was bringing the divorce up now, out of the blue, it seemed to her. Then, as her mind slowly made the connection between James believing her a slut and talking divorce, she flushed searingly and hurriedly turned her head away.

'That's what you want, isn't it? Your freedom? What you've been wanting for ages, even before you walked out on me. I've been a fool not believing you meant it, for thinking that, for all our misunderstandings about your career and my business, we still cared enough about each other to try and resolve things. But I've been wrong— all along the line, it seems.' James's voice was detached and, when Roz could bring herself to look at him again, his eyes were as detached as his voice as he contemplated her across the small room. It might have been a chasm between them.

'It was only me doing the caring. You never really cared about me at all. I see that now.' Amazingly, James smiled at her and looked quite pleased with his own awful conclusion. Roz shrank into herself. 'The man you cared about, Rosalind—and that was only in the beginning— was some fantasy guy in your head, who supposedly came swashbuckling into your life on a white charger and swept you off your feet. And then he was supposed to be forever romantic and sexy and keep whisking you off to bed every other minute to prove how ravishingly desirable you were.' James caught back the derisive guffaw that had involuntarily grated out. 'God knows I tried to match up to your fantasy, Rosalind, more fool me! But I'm only human, and when reality couldn't be put off any longer and I turned into an ordinary, busy, worried man trying to keep his business together... when I was too dead on my feet to play my assigned role of the perfect husband in your fantasy of a perfect marriage, you didn't want to know. I'd fluffed it, and you turned your back on me and went your own way.'

Roz sat turned to stone by this fantastic version of their time together. James went on, a weary bitterness threading his voice. 'Well, I hope you're going to be happy in your chosen way— with your career and your lovers—but count me out for good now, Rosalind,' James told her. And, for the first time since he began his appalling account, anger showed in his eyes. 'Oh, yes, I did want us to try again, and would have settled happily for a lot of compromise in a not-so-perfect marriage, but now that you've made so clear the only thing you want from me is a "roll in the hay"—I quote—whenever the urge takes you, then, thick as I've been, I know it's finally over between us. I'll have to pass on your offer in that quarter, I'm afraid. I'm not so hung-up on you that I'm prepared to trade in my self-respect and stand in a queue for a night in your arms.'

CHAPTER EIGHT

IF HER life had depended on it at that moment, Roz could not have managed a word of protest in her own self-defence. She felt stupid with horror at the unbelievable things James had said, and could only watch dumbly as he walked to the door. When he turned to her, her mind was not capable of anything more than a dull curiosity as to what else he could possibly have left to say, when surely by now he must have exhausted his storehouse of lacerating home truths.

'I'm very busy at the office these days. Yes, I know you've heard that before, but I give you my word I will be in touch with the solicitor about the divorce before the end of the week—if I have to ring him at midnight,' James promised—or threatened; it was all one.

'Fine,' Roz heard herself reply, almost gaily.

'I'm sure it is, since you'll be getting what you've been working so hard for.' James pulled the corners of his mouth up in a grim jerk. 'But you needn't lose any sleep about your reputation, because I don't think I'll bring your adulteries into the proceedings. I rather have a fancy to play your fantasy hero to the last and allow you to divorce me . . . on those grounds you mentioned. What was the term now?' James furrowed his brow in mock concentration. 'Ah, yes, *my* unreasonable behaviour, wasn't it?' His eyes ranged over her coldly and slowly, as if he was taking his final, distasteful look at her and committing her waxen face to memory. For a split second, the eyes flashed pain before James shrugged away whatever it was that had fleetingly strayed into his mind and the gaze turned to ice again. 'Congratulations Rosalind. You've won.'

Roz sobbed herself to sleep, and in the morning woke feeling sick and still haunted by the image of James's face exuding the dreadful contempt that made her want to shrivel up and die. That he actually believed her capable of diving in and out of bed with any man who crossed her path was monstrous, regardless of what lies she had told or implied about herself. But what was more shattering was the vicious picture James had presented of her as a shallow, self-centred and uncaring wife; that was more cruel than any aspersions on her morals. And untrue.

She had never expected James to be a perfect husband, whatever that meant, and if she hadn't been as supportive as she might have been it was only because James had never let on that he had worries or needed her support. And now he was turning on her and...

The utter unfairness of his accusations pushed the hurt out of the way and brought on such a rush of self-righteous anger that Roz wanted to storm off to Allied Press there and then and yell her own version of home truths at him—that he was not the only one to think himself badly done by. What about all those months he had virtually disappeared out of her life—rarely home, and when he was he had been a sullen, uncommunicative stranger? Didn't James realise how insecure and scared he had made her feel before the defensive indifference set in, when she put two and two together and came up with other women? Maybe, just maybe, she had been wrong about that, but the damage had been done and there was no turning back the clock.

And there was no point now in storming off to his office and railing at him. James was going to give her the divorce she had wanted—still wanted, Roz corrected herself hastily. No more fuzzy confusions now, no more irrational wavering about whether they should try to make another go of it. *Finito.* Over. She could get on with her future. Alone. And if she didn't become one of the best photographers in the business it wouldn't be for want of trying—or single-mindedness. Move over, Lyn Barrett!

Roz laughed aloud on a sudden charge of adrenalin that shot her up to a piercing high, and if she was aware of a slightly manic quality to her activities during the following days, she assured herself it was simply long-suppressed energy allowed its head at last. Life had never been more exhilarating: freedom from James was around the corner, the Famine Relief Agency's fund-raising night was coming up on Saturday, when her photographs would prove to be a feather in her professional cap, the next exciting project was already lined up and waiting for her. What more could she ask for?

'I've never seen you like this, Roz. Did you win the Pools or something?' Lyn asked with an uneasy laugh when they were having a coffee in Lyn's kitchen on the Thursday, after the Relief Agency's publicity officer had carted away the collection of Roz's Zangyrian photographs.

'Not quite,' Roz dismissed Lyn's ill-disguised concern on a flare of irritation, aware that Lyn had been observing her more and more curiously each day. 'I just feel great. Anything wrong with that?'

'No. No, of course not,' Lyn assured her hurriedly. 'I just wondered... You don't want to talk about anything, do you?' Lyn persisted.

Her question made Roz snap immediately, 'Only about work.' And then, feeling a little churlish, she added brightly, 'I can't get enough of it.'

She had spend most of the week with Lyn and the publicity officer, seeing to the last details of the fund-raising exhibition, and at home, going through literally hundreds of photographs, trying to get an updated portfolio together for Lyn, and generally keeping so busy that at the end of each day she was able to fall into bed in an exhausted heap, blanking out the moment her head hit the pillow and with no stretch of time in between for her thoughts to stray to James. During the days, everything was so tightly locked away deep inside her that Roz felt hermetically sealed from emotions, safe and secure, and riding her exhilaration like a surfer on an enormous, wonderful wave, until late Friday afternoon when the wave hit shore and plummeted her down from the high.

The phone rang and Roz answered it with a cheerful 'Yes, hello,' safe in the knowledge that the voice on the other end of the line would never again be James's.

'Mrs Thornton?'

'Yes,' agreed Roz, unable to place the crisp female voice.

'Thompson, Willis and Barclay here,' the woman rattled off the string of names, which could only have meant solicitors, but didn't mean a thing to Roz at that moment.

'Mr Willis is on the line to speak to you, Mrs Thornton.'

'Who?'

'Mr Willis, your solicitor. I'm putting him on now.'

Afterwards, Roz couldn't get over herself acting so stunned when David Willis told her, as cheerfully as his professional reticence allowed, that all her problems were over and he had only just that day received communication from Mr Thornton's solicitors to say that their client would no longer stand in the way of an early divorce, and wasn't that wonderful? He didn't quite put it that way. He said something like, 'I'm sure you'll be very pleased and relieved, Mrs Thornton.' Roz said that yes, she was, and wondered why she felt so shocked when she had been expecting to receive that sort of news. By letter, granted, in a week or two—she was sure James would carry out his word—but for several numbing moments she felt as if the urbane Mr Willis had sprung the biggest shock of her life on her.

'We'll be in touch with you by letter, of course, but I thought I'd let you know immediately because I knew how happy it would make you.' Mr Willis's voice asked for a pat on the back for his thoughtfulness.

'Thank you. That was very kind of you,' Roz responded mechanically and, putting the phone down, realised that she was shaking. So much for jumping in the air, clicking her heels, as she had gaily envisaged herself doing when word finally came through. Word had come through and she felt sick to the stomach and would have given anything to beg off going to the fund-raising the next night. But she felt too down to begin to think of an excuse that Lyn wouldn't override, and in the end didn't even try. She went, dressed in the ubiquitous cashmere wool, looking ultra-elegant and feeling as flat as a pricked balloon.

Overall, Roz supposed the night was a success. For one thing, having been sent Press releases about the celebrities due to put in an appearance, the media had turned up in droves and the Agency's organisers were thrilled to bits.

The photographs provided a not-very-discreet background to the evening's proceedings, but then discretion was not the name of the game when you wanted people to dip into their pockets, only Roz couldn't help noticing that, after an obligatory sweep of the eye over them, nobody really looked at the photographs again if they could help it. She wondered why the agency had gone to the trouble, not to mention the expense, of acquiring them.

Roz mingled diligently and wished she could go home. The crush and chatter were getting on her nerves, with the evening taking on the air of a large, noisy party once the official programme had been got out of the way. There had been a couple of short talks given by decent, non-glamorous relief workers, followed by a very heartwarming plea for funds by the guest celebrity—a film star whose overpowering glamour and dangerously dipping *décolletage* had the press cameras flashing and TV cameras rolling non-stop, and at least ensuring a mention of the Agency's name in the next day's news. After that came the buffet supper, with some frankly dreadful wine that went to the head in double-quick time, lightening the mood of the evening as it went. That was when Roz started wanting to go home.

It was a relief, and not a moment too soon, when Lyn materialised at her side to hiss for all the world to hear that she'd had enough and how about they clear off?

'God, those things are a bore, aren't they? Your photos came up great though, didn't they?' Lyn threw herself into the driver's seat and began grinding the cold engine into reluctant life.

'For what they were worth—and that wasn't much,' Roz muttered sarcastically under her breath.

About to give the ignition key another wrench, Lyn flung her a glance. 'Yes, it can all be a bit of an anticlimax in the end. I've been there, too, you know.' Lyn could be perceptive when she chose. 'Never mind——' she raised her voice above the clatter of the motor which stayed chugging and set them off at last '—at least it's all over. You can slap a few more photos into your portfolio and get on with the next job. Versatility is what you need to aim at at this stage of your career. By the way, I didn't see any sign of that husband of yours, did you?' She tossed in the surprising question apropos of nothing, and had Roz racking her brains as to why Lyn could have possibly expected James, of all people, to show up.

In the end, she asked edgily, 'What made you think James might come?'

'Well, he did ask to be sent an invitation.' Lyn ignored the edge, or didn't notice it. 'That day when he turned up at the studio before you, you remember. So I passed on the message to the Agency people and assumed they sent him one, and that he'd show up—to see your work all set up professionally and all that, if not to shell out money. But I dare say he's got other things on his mind at the moment.'

Roz made an odd cackling noise in her throat. 'You're right there. Divorce. James has agreed to it. The solicitor rang me about it yesterday to confirm. So you see, I, for one, did not expect to see "that husband of mine" this evening.'

She had not intended to tell Lyn anything about the forthcoming divorce until proceedings were well in progress, but telling her now was as good a way as any of putting an end to Lyn's infuriating curiosity and silly projections of imagination.

'Well, well!' Lyn exclaimed softly. 'So it has finally come to that.' She chewed her lower lip mercilessly and drove on in short-lived silence. 'But do you really want a divorce, Roz?' Swinging her face round suddenly, she tried to get Roz to meet her eyes in the semi-darkness.

'Do keep your eyes on the road, for heaven's sake!' Roz snapped in alarm. 'Yes, of course I want a divorce. I've been wanting one ever since I left him, and James is being sensible about it at last, which is why I've been so insufferably cheerful all week, if you must know.'

'Good old James,' Lyn said tartly. 'That'll keep him out of mischief—along with everything else. I can't say I ever liked your James, Roz; he's always been too much the super-arrogant male for my tastes, but I must confess to feeling a teensy bit sorry for him now, with everybody gunning for him from all sides. I'm not surprised, either, that he's throwing in one towel after another—or is it sponge?' Lyn chuckled. 'I always get them mixed up.'

Roz frowned, trying to make sense of Lyn's ramblings. 'I wish you wouldn't exaggerate so much, Lyn. Wanting to divorce someone is hardly gunning for them,' she pointed out irritably, 'and talking to a solicitor once or twice is not exactly going to take up twenty-four hours of James's day for months on end.'

'I'm not talking about the divorce, I'm talking about all that takeover business. What's James going to do now that he's out on his ear?'

'Out on his ear?' Roz repeated like a surprised parrot.

Lyn tinkled out a careless laugh. 'Well, that's what usually happens when you get taken over, isn't it? You get turfed out. I'm no expert, but Peter has been quite interested in all the machinations behind the scenes, following Allied Press's struggles off and on. And he says James will have to go—they always do, apparently. From the sound of it, though, I imagine James will be quite relieved to take his money and run. I know I would be—not that you'd catch me dead in a no-win set-up like that to start off with. I've got better things to do with my life than fight unions and boards and takeover sharks. What a life!' Lyn gave an exaggerated shudder as she swung the car in towards the kerb outside Roz's house and scraped the tyres jarringly against the kerb while she was at it. 'Oops, sorry!' She brought the car to a halt but kept the engine running. 'Anyway, I just wondered what his plans were now. Curiosity. You know me, I'm horrible with it.'

Things were coming together very slowly in Roz's dazed mind: Allied Press had been taken over, James was to be out on his ear, but more dazing than that was that Lyn knew all about it and *she* didn't. 'How do you know all this?' Roz managed to get the amazed thought into words.

Momentarily startled, Lyn looked at her strangely, then burst out laughing. 'Good heavens, Roz, don't tell me you didn't know about the takeover?'

'No. Yes...' Roz flushed guiltily, and was glad the colour couldn't show up in the light of the streetlamps across the road. It was too mortifying to admit that the little she had known about a takeover in the offing she had dismissed, without bothering to get the right end of the stick as to who was taking over whom, and now her mind had to do all manner of mental gymnastics to take in the incredible fact that Allied Press— James—had been the actual target of the takeover.

'The business pages have been full of it for ages,' Lyn informed her offhandedly. 'Not that I read them—any more than you do, it seems. Peter does though, and yesterday, after James gave in to his board and let that Canadian newspaper piranha, McGinley, have Allied Press, the affair actually rated a column or two on the front page of some of the papers. My guess is so they could feature a picture of McGinley's glitzy wife in full war-paint. Not a very good pic, either. Most of my first-year-students could have done better.'

Roz wasn't listening; she couldn't any more. Didn't Lyn realise what she was trilling on about? James's whole life had been turned upside-down, and all Lyn could think of was the quality of the photo of somebody's wife! 'Thanks for the lift, Lyn,' Roz said abruptly and jumped out of the car.

'I'll be in touch,' Lyn yelled, revving the engine excruciatingly, then setting the battered vehicle off with a jump.

It was too late to go out and buy some newspapers; Roz didn't doubt that what Lyn had told her was essentially true, but Lyn was prone to such extravagant exaggeration that it was hard to tell where fact left off and embellishment began. Surely James wouldn't be out on his ear? Things like that didn't happen. Or did they? Roz wished she had more insight into business in general, and James's in particular. She wished, too, that she had been more persistent when she had tried to break through James's barrier at Cecily's and at least managed to get some basic facts out of him.

Not that she could have changed anything; but she might have acted differently later—Monday night, for instance, when James had waited all that time to see her. He'd said it was primarily to discuss their relationship, but he must have needed to talk to her about other things, too. Needed her, full stop—as he had needed her in the course of all those earlier business hassles she had never known about. Instead, in the middle of his latest drama at work, she had driven him to the point of giving up on the marriage he had so grimly hung on to. The timing could not have been worse! Roz tried to imagine how she would be feeling in James's place now, and made herself shudder.

A glance at her watch showed ten past eleven. Late, but not that late. The thought that was forming in her head terrified her. After the horrid events of Monday night, she was probably the last person James wanted to talk to.

Roz dithered irresolutely in the corridor, then quickly, before she could give herself time to change her mind, ran to the telephone and called a cab. She went outside to wait for it, shivering with cold, but afraid to stay inside in case her nerve failed her and she cancelled the cab and backed out of making the one last gesture that might soften the hard-edged picture James had of her as a selfish, uncaring wife. There was no way she could change what she had been, but she'd be able to like herself a little bit more if she made the trip to James now, and told him simply that she cared about what had happened to him and that there was no need to hurry with the divorce if he had other more pressing things to attend to.

She put together a few simple, sincere sentences and mentally rehearsed them in the cab, only to have them disappear completely from her head when James opened the door to her and looked as if he was having trouble working out who she was, let alone what she was doing on his doorstep at quarter to twelve on a Saturday night. Unnerved, Roz cast a frantic glance behind her and saw the tail-lights of the cab already blinking half-way down the block.

'What are you doing here, Rosalind?'

He had worked out who she was, that was a start. Roz wished she could tell him what she was doing here, but for the moment it seemed as much a mystery to her as to James. She stared inanely into his frowning face. Nothing about James matched up with her wildly melodramatic picture of a broken man; he looked as he had always looked of late—terse and tired, and, right now, so intimidating that she felt paralysed with apprehensiveness.

'You'd better come in,' James said at last, grudgingly. He stood aside to let her pass, his frown intensifying as Roz stayed rooted to the doorstep.

Go away now, she ordered herself, bolt for it before you make a bigger fool of yourself. James does not need you. Ignoring her own advice, Roz stepped into the hall.

James led her into the front reception room. The room was cold and she shivered. 'Is anything the matter, Rosalind?' The sharpness in the voice might have been brusque concern, but might have been plain annoyance, too, at having his time wasted by his soon-to-be-ex-wife turning up at midnight and not being able to utter a single word of explanation.

Roz took it as the latter and hurriedly summoned up a smile which must have been positively brilliant; she could feel her mouth stretching from ear to ear. 'Oh, no, nothing. I was on my way home from the Relief Agency's fund-raising night and saw the lights on, so I thought I'd drop in. It was just around the corner from here...' Give or take a mile or three. 'It was a super night. Everybody was there, and my photos were a great success...' What was she raving about? This was not how she meant to start. It was awful—prattling about herself.

James was regarding her strangely. She couldn't blame him for that. 'Congratulations,' he said coldly, and it was like having a bucket of water thrown over her. The mad bravado fizzled out in an instant.

Grimacing, Roz gave a frustrated shake of her head. 'I didn't come to tell... I came... How are you, James?' She flung the question at him desperately.

James seemed to consider the question for ages. 'Fine,' he replied carefully, and Roz could almost hear his mind ticking over, trying to work out what was going on. 'Is that what you came to ask me, Rosalind?' A faintly sardonic smile flickered at the corners of James's mouth.

Roz flushed and looked away. It was exactly what she had come to ask, and to tell him she cared. Back at her flat, it had sounded reasonable. And simple. 'I'm sorry; I care,' the words were still in her head, only there didn't seem any way she could get them out of there, and James was not making it any easier for her. Roz brought her eyes to him again. 'I heard this evening... about Allied Press.' She paused as James's dark brows shot together into a discouraging peak, then struggled on. 'You know... about the takeover.' Did James understand what she was trying to say? Roz could tell nothing from the closed-up and closed-off expression, and did not know how to go on in the face of it. But, having made the gesture, however impetuously, she had to persevere now, because in her mind the gesture was assuming monumental proportions, and getting through to James was taking on an irrational life and death importance. 'I thought we could talk about it— if you wanted to, that is,' she offered quickly, and then, realising she'd left herself open to receiving a blunt 'no, thanks', ran on frantically to keep up a flow of words—any words—until she talked herself into some sort of rationality. 'I know it's a funny hour to turn up, but I didn't come before because I didn't know about what had happened...what was happening. It must have been so awful for you, and I...You don't have to push the divorce through now if you're too busy, it's not important. Oh, James, why didn't you tell me?' Everything was coming out disjointedly, all over the place. Roz didn't know what she was saying, yet something must have been getting through to James. She followed the changes in his expression, from the distancing iciness to the puzzlement, to the wavering comprehension.

And then James seemed trapped by indecision. He threw a glance at the door, all at once distracted and on edge. 'Will you wait here for a few minutes while I attend to something? Please, Rosalind.' The new note of urgency sounded like her own. 'I want us to talk, I really do, only you've caught me at a bad moment, so if you could just wait ... make yourself at home, pour yourself a drink, turn on the heating,' James was practically babbling in what seemed frantic haste to get himself out of the room, only he didn't quite make it.

'James, where are you? What's keeping you?' a female voice called out from just outside the room. A moment later, Barbara Russell materialised in the doorway.

Roz's eyes flew back to James, who was trapped near the door, and then to the secretary again, taking in every detail at lightning speed: Ms Russell's hair was loose around her shoulders, making her look far prettier than Roz remembered her; she was wearing slacks and a sweater, a casual, up-to-the-minute style with the deep V at the front which was designed for sexiness, not warmth. Roz didn't need a crystal ball to tell her what the secretary was doing in James's house on a Saturday night; one educated guess and the embarrassed flush on the woman's face told all, not to speak of James's own stricken look.

'I think you've met Barbara, my secretary.' James barely moved his lips and sounded as if he was choking.

Roz felt hot and cold, mortified and furious— with herself. 'Yes, of course,' she trilled, super-graciously in a curious falsetto, amazing herself that words could actually come out of her mouth at all; it must have been pure reflex. She prayed she would sink through the floor. 'How are you,

Barbara?' she went on to enquire, like a charming hostess greeting a favourite guest.

'Barbara has been helping me with some business details,' James mumbled, not looking at either of the women. 'We've finished now, and Barbara was about to leave.'

Roz tinkled out a high-pitched laugh. 'Nonsense, James, you must carry on! You should have told me you were entertaining. I wouldn't have dreamt of disturbing you,' Roz addressed him with the same grotesquely arch politeness and sailed blindly to the door. 'We can talk divorce another time, when you're not so busy,' she tossed her parting shot at him, injecting it with all the malice she could muster.

James hadn't moved an inch and looked as if he had been turned to stone. Roz smiled, or at least felt her mouth twisting into *something* before she pushed past the secretary and fled the room.

'Rosalind, wait!' James called the urgent order after her as she tore down the hall, her face on fire, the rest of her ice-cold and trembling.

He must have come to life the instant she was out of the room, for he caught up with her at the front door. Grabbing her arm, he spun her around to him. 'We were working, Rosalind. I swear that was all. There is nothing going on between Barbara and myself. Nothing,' he repeated forcefully.

The drawing-room door closed with a soft click, with Barbara Russell remaining in the room.

Roz looked past James's shoulder to the discreetly closed door. 'It's not my business, James. You can do what you like, with whomever you choose to do it with. I don't care,' she said, almost loftily, in the attempt to hang on to her trembling dignity.

'You do care!' James contradicted fiercely. 'You must, or you wouldn't be acting like this. You wouldn't have come here to see me in the first place if you hadn't cared about me. Don't go back on your feelings now, Rosalind. We can sort all this out. You want to; I want to,' James pleaded in harsh, desperate anger.

'No!' Roz shook her head wildly and, twisting out of his grip, wrenched open the door and ran out of the house.

Luck was with her in the form of a cab depositing its passengers across the road from James's house. Roz was across the road and in the cab as James came flying down the steps. 'Please hurry,' she begged the undisturbed driver, to whom a distraught woman chased by a man might have been nothing more than par for the course in his line of business.

Fool, fool, fool! Roz berated herself all the way home. She was still cursing herself as she lay in bed, staring dismally up at the ceiling in the darkness, with the humiliation still as sharp and stinging as the moment Barbara Russell had showed herself in the doorway and everything had fallen into place.

Barbara Russell. Why not? Caught out, James had lied about her, coming out with the first pa-

thetic explanation to stumble off his tongue—
business. And the rest! Roz doubted she'd have
managed anything better in his place, but how
could she have been so naïve as not to have suspected something was going on between them?
Bosses and secretaries were a trite duo, but a very
sensible combination if you thought about it. Roz
thought about it, with an aching despair and a
dull, hopeless acceptance. She couldn't blame
James for turning to the woman when he needed
to have someone who understood what he was
going through. Barbara Russell was the ideal
candidate—at his side every step of the way,
knowing every detail of the takeover struggle and
James's last-ditch fight against it, and being able
to provide the support he needed, and which Roz
herself had only just realised he had needed. Too
late.

It was incredible that it had taken so long for
it to sink through that she did care, passionately,
about James, their marriage and their future.
And to realise she didn't want a divorce any more,
but a reconciliation. Her subconscious had
known it, sending her flying into the night to tell
James just that, and now every fibre of her consciousness knew it, too; with the same certainty
that it knew she had lost him—ironically, to the
'other woman' she had been so afraid of right
from the start. Not specifically Barbara Russell;
the woman of her jealous fantasies had never had
a name, but had always been there, none the less,
casting a threatening shadow over Roz's life when
the tenor of her marriage had started to change

and she hadn't been able to grow up quickly enough to cope with it.

The silly, naïve girl she had been had latched on to the standard scapegoat to account for her own inadequacies, and to blame for the end of the long honeymoon. A perfect marriage, James had accused her of wanting, and when she couldn't have it she had left, instead of reaching out and trying to talk through her feelings about James's work, her career, her needs, James's needs. Compromise was the word and James had used it, whereas, locked into her immature idealism, Roz had never known what it meant. Or could mean.

Nothing had changed in the morning; her mood was still bleak and flat and grey, and everything around seemed to have gone out of its way to match it: the flat looked bleaker than it ever looked, outside, the sky looked an uncompromising grey. Roz mooched about all morning, restless and listless, and then in the afternoon got herself out of the flat in a flurry and set off for Cecily's because, other than Lyn's, she couldn't think where else to go and was afraid that, if she didn't take herself off somewhere, and fast, she might just land up on James's doorstep again, begging him to take her back, or something equally mortifying. And her pride had taken enough of a battering at the sight of Barbara Russell last night. Roz's imagination couldn't stretch the length to project how she would feel if desperation drove her to James now, and she found Ms Russell still swanning about.

The train journey was soothing in its tediousness. There was something about long train trips that deadened the mind and shut out reality as one rattled along past anonymous towns and fields, sitting in a carriage full of anonymous people who knew nothing about you and could not have cared less.

The cab that sometimes bothered to meet the train was nowhere about, and the bus that serviced the village during the week did not run on Sundays. Roz started walking. Cecily would have sent Matthew to pick her up if she had known Roz was coming, but Roz had deliberately not telephoned, not wanting to alarm the old lady into reading all sorts of dire meaning into another visit so soon after last Sunday's.

Was it only a week ago? Time had become confused in Roz's head; it seemed for ever since she and James had spent the night in each other's arms in the pub she was just passing. And it seemed, too, that she had been alone for ever, with part of her missing, an emptiness no career could make up for. If only she had listened to her heart then, instead of trying to rationalise their lovemaking away, too stubborn and too scared to admit to herself that yes, she did love James and needed him back in her life.

Roz marched on glumly, and then, to her relief, she spotted the village cab. It was turning into the High Street from the side street behind her father's former shop, just ahead of her. She darted on to the road and semaphored wildly with her hands, bringing old Mr Willow to a startled, bumpy stop. His eyesight was a lot better than his driving, and he recognised her immediately and, anticipating her destination, executed an ungainly U-turn that had Roz flattening herself quickly against a shop window as one wheel rode up the kerb. Only in a time-forgotten village like this could you get away with being a cab driver at Mr Willow's never-referred-to age, thought Roz with genuine fondness as she clambered in. She felt safer in the vehicle than out of it, enjoying the gently grumbling commentary on the sad state of the world all the way to Cecily's.

CHAPTER NINE

LUCY answered the door, and the pleasantly bland expression she always wore over the criss-cross of wrinkles seized up a little when she saw it was Roz.

'Oh! Mrs Thornton. Good afternoon, madam.' She resorted to formality, which she only did when she was nervous, and that was not often. Then she stood there, at a loss, like a house-keeper on stage who had forgotten her next line.

Nonplussed by the odd reception, Roz smiled uneasily. 'Hello, Lucy. Yes, it's me. I thought I'd just drop by to see Mrs Thornton again,' she returned with a stab at being casual, and thought how stupid she sounded. Lucy was not particularly bright, but she was not so dense she couldn't work out that when someone lived in London they didn't just 'drop by' into the middle of Norfolk without going to quite a lot of trouble to do it.

The old housekeeper looked as if she had every intention of leaving her on the doorstep, so, taking the initiative, Roz stepped briskly into the hall. 'Mrs Thornton is in, isn't she?'

'Yes. Upstairs. In bed.' The information was transmitted in reluctant jerks and set off alarm bells in Roz's head.

'Is everything all right? She's not unwell?'

Lucy shook her head stolidly. 'Just taking a rest.'

Roz let out a little laugh of relief. 'I rather feel I could do with one myself after rattling on the train for so long. Then I had to walk half-way to the village before Mr Willow came by,' she rattled on, overdoing the chatter in her discomfort. 'Any chance of a cup of tea?' Roz started towards the smaller drawing-room, the one they had used last Sunday, and had to pull up abruptly as Lucy sort of flung herself in front of her and yanked open the door they were just passing, which happened to be to the main, formal drawing-room and which Cecily rarely used.

'Wouldn't you prefer tea in here, Mrs Thornton?' She smiled a peculiarly ingratiating smile that had Roz completely baffled, and not a little irritated.

'No, thank you, Lucy. The terrace room will be fine,' she said sternly and frowned at the old lady. 'Lucy, what on earth has got into you? You don't seem at all yourself. Are you sure everything is all right?'

Lucy muttered something under her breath that Roz did not catch, and closed the door of the room she had been trying to tempt Roz into with a piqued little bang, saying in a resigned, put-upon voice, 'As you wish, madam. I shall bring the tea to the terrace room.'

'Please do.' Frankly amazed, Roz stood watching her clack loudly down the tessellated hall until Lucy turned into the corridor to the kitchen. Then, her curiosity well and truly aroused, she hurried into the terrace room and looked about suspiciously, to see what it was that Lucy hadn't wanted her to see.

Her eyes ranged over the fire in the grate, casting its warm glow over the comfortable, mellow room: Cecily's embroidery was in its familiar position in the corner of a settee; vases of flowers brightened the room from various side tables. There was nothing remotely out of the ordinary, and certainly no evidence of anything as exotically outlandish as Lucy running an illegal gambling den, which Roz's imagination had wildly started to conjure up. More perplexed than ever, she went over to the fire and held her hands to it, frowning into the flames.

The first thing Lucy did when she clattered in with the tray was dart her eyes sharply around the room, only she seemed surprised, rather than reassured by what she saw—or didn't see. She put the tray down on the coffee-table without a word.

'Thank you, Lucy,' said Roz politely, and then noticed the two cups on the tray. 'Is Mrs Thornton coming down now?'

'No,' Lucy returned bluntly and looked pointedly at the french windows, as if they held the answer to anything Roz might want to know. 'If there's nothing else, madam...'

'No, thank you.' Roz was finding the old housekeeper a strain on the nerves.

She sprang to the windows the moment Lucy was out of the room and, looking out over the

terrace, understood instantly why the second cup
was on the tray, and why Lucy had acted so
strangely and had wanted her to use the other
room—the room James was not using. Without
Cecily to instruct her, poor old Lucy had been
thrown into a dither at having an estranged
husband and wife turning up independently, and
her social skills had not been up to it. The best
she could think of was putting them into separate rooms—probably with the idea of locking
the door on each of them!

James was sitting on a stone urn at the foot of
the terrace, staring into space. Roz was not
shocked to see him; she was not surprised, and
not glad, because it hurt just to look at him. She
did not know how she felt. As she watched,
James turned slowly towards the windows, as if
sensing her eyes on him. While reason told her
the distance between them was too great for
actual eye contact, Roz felt their eyes lock for an
interminable moment and was conscious of a
spasm of undefined hope and a brief sense of
expectation before James turned away again. The
churn of disappointment was as surprising as the
irrational feelings that had preceded it. What had
she hoped or expected? That James would spring
up and come running up the terrace to her and
gather her up in his arms in the final cliché of
romantic fantasy? Roz supposed so, and felt bitterly angry at herself for having been clinging,
even subconsciously, to such a hopeless cop-out
in the face of reality.

The reality was that James had finished with her once and for all; he had Barbara Russell now, and wanted a divorce, and he had come to his mother's house to get himself a break and not have his Sunday spoilt by his wife turning up like the proverbial bad penny. Roz felt as embarrassed as if she had tailed him here, and the most pressing thought in her mind as she slipped out of the room and ran down the terrace was to tell him it wasn't so, that she hadn't come looking for him, and it was simply unhappy coincidence that had drawn her to Cecily's, too.

'I'm sorry,' she started blurting breathlessly before she even reached him. 'I wouldn't have come if I'd known you were here.'

James had not turned to look at her approach; he continued staring across the expanse of lawn, giving no sign that he had heard her, but he must have because, just when Roz was about to repeat herself, he said flatly, 'No, I don't suppose you would have.'

She didn't know what to say next in the silence that followed. A flat, dispirited silence, as drained of life as James's voice, and everything else about him—as she herself had felt, and probably looked too. But, instead of sympathy, empathy, or whatever, what Roz felt was a stir of anger that this was how everything was going to end between them—fade away with a tired, jaded old whimper.

The anger sharpened. It wouldn't end like this if she could help it; she would rather they hurled abuse one last time and stormed off, hurt and furious and hating each other, but at least knowing they were alive; anything but this half-dead emotional vacuum. Roz said, a little scared, but knowing exactly what she was doing and why, 'And did you finish attending to all those important business details I so indiscreetly interrupted you and Ms Russell at last night?' Her voice held just the right amount of snakiness and disbelief, and she had a tremor of satisfaction at seeing James's jaw go into a sudden clench as the barb pierced home.

He swung his eyes to her in a glare. She looked back, mocking and all bland innocence.

'Yes, we did,' James ground out through his teeth.

'Oh, I'm so glad,' Roz gushed. 'I was afraid I might have put you off your stride, or whatever the term is.' She smiled coyly, noting the anger fusing colour into James's face, and his eyes narrowing and sizing her up, like a boxer facing an unknown challenger. A pulse quickened nervously in her throat, Roz kept her tacky little smile in place, waiting for James's anger to come to full life.

'What are you fishing for, Rosalind? The lurid details?' James curled up his top lip at her in a gleaming snarl, and his eyes flashed sparks that hadn't been there a moment ago, but Roz's triumph at putting them there was short-lived as he sprang up without warning. 'Is that what you'd like me to tell you about? All the lovely lurid details?' James asked, suggestively, and Roz would never have believed he could actually leer like that.

'No, thanks,' she muttered, quite shocked, and backed several hasty steps away from him, alarmed at the unexpected turn her needling had taken.

'But why not, Rosalind? Surely your feminine curiosity has been torturing you all night. Didn't you spend half the night lying awake imagining what Barbara and I were doing, and how long we had been at it?' James positively purred malice at her. 'Shall I fill in the gaps for you now?'

Roz shook her head agitatedly.

'Oh, that's only your natural delicacy.' James waved a hand dismissively. 'Let's dispense with that for the moment, shall we? I'm going to tell you all about Barbara and me, because I know you're simply dying to know all about us, and you've probably already guessed it wasn't the first night Barbara and I had spent together. There, I've admitted it. Satisfied?' James smiled tauntingly. Roz went a burning red and didn't know where to look. She dropped her eyes down to the paving stones under her feet, fixing on the small patch of moss in the crack at the edge of her shoe.

'Yes, we've spent a lot of nights together lately,' James went on reminiscently, and with relish, it seemed to Roz's appalled ears. 'Barbara has been simply wonderful, really supportive and understanding. I honestly don't know how I would have managed without her.'

James was voicing her own despairing conclusions aloud, and enjoying doing it. She had deliberately goaded him into bringing the subject of Barbara Russell out into the open, anticipating angry denials, accusations and counter-accusations, but hadn't for a moment expected James would want to humiliate her like this. Roz wanted to block her ears; she kept her eyes down, squirming with mortification.

'And now for those indelicate details you've been itching to hear about...' James's enjoyment was edging nastily close to cruelty. 'Let me see, there were twenty-four...'

Roz jerked her head up in horrified interest.

'Yes, you heard right,' James confirmed with a savage grin. 'Twenty-four people on Allied Press's new proprietor's hit list—mainly chaps who've been with Allied Press for decades and are considered past their prime. And they probably are, but by working at it in our spare time over the last couple of weeks—and that includes a lot of nights—Barbara and I have been able to draw up a list of possible jobs for them to start looking into when the new brooms begin sweeping them out into the street like so much dead wood. We were burning the midnight oil over the last four, very hard-to-place cases when you arrived and caught us red-handed.'

The macabre game was over and, too stunned to fully take in what James had just told her, Roz was truly frightened of the rage in his face. She yelped with shock and pain as his hands grabbed her shoulders and shook her like a lifeless rag doll.

'You couldn't see for the green spots in front of your eyes last night, let alone hear anything I might have had to say. But did you really care, Rosalind, or was it all blind jealous rage?' James hissed at her. 'Do you care about me—about us? Do you? Was that what you came to tell me last night? Tell me! Was it?' Violence surged out through James's voice and through the hands kneading viciously into her shoulders, like those of a masseur gone mad.

Roz looked at him desperately and nodded silently, and was incapable of telling whether the flash in James's eyes was relief, belief or simply satisfaction at having bullied the mute confession out of her at last.

He released her suddenly and drew back, facing her with his hands clenching and unclenching at his sides. 'Then, for God's sake, what was last Monday night all about, when you told me all we had going for us was sex?' James yelled at a volume that Lucy must have heard from the house, and Cecily, too—and anybody else this side of the village. This was washing dirty linen in public with a vengeance.

Roz clamped her teeth into her lower lip and tasted blood.

'And all those lovers! How do you think that made me feel?'

'I lied,' Roz whispered.

James barked out a laugh. 'I knew that—or, at least, I figured it out later. But why? Why did you do it? Tell me that.'

'I don't know,' she was almost whimpering. 'To pay you back for...I don't know...for making me so mixed up.' Roz was not making much sense even to herself. James was glowering at her—incredulous, impatient. She tried again. 'You were so...smug...' Wrong word. 'You...you took so much for granted—that I didn't want a divorce any more, and I wasn't sure myself what I...' How could she explain something that was so irrational and utterly beyond explanation?

The fists had stopped their clenching, and an unreassuring calm appeared to have settled over James as he stared at her. 'Do you or do you not want a divorce, Rosalind?' he asked, enunciating slowly and carefully, as if he was speaking to someone of very limited intelligence.

'I...'

'Yes or no,' he snapped her off with a bite, and could have passed for one of those barristers who make a living frightening witnesses to death.

'No, but...'

'Oh, my God, here we go again!' James made a clutch at his head, contorting his face into an ugly grimace. '"No, but...yes, but..."' he mimicked grotesquely. 'I can't stand it any more. So help me, I'm going out of my mind trying to work out what you mean. Can't you for once, just once, say something and actually mean it without equivocating like mad in the next breath? I asked you whether you want a divorce.'

'I said no and I meant it, but you didn't let me finish.' Roz's voice gathered strength. 'I wanted to say that I thought it was you who wanted the divorce now. After all the things you said, I...'

'I said a lot of things that night that I didn't mean,' James cut in hurriedly, flustered all at once.

'And some that you did,' Roz pointed out heatedly. James flushed and shrugged, but had the honesty not to deny it. 'And some were damned unfair and not true,' she lashed out on an unexpected wave of anger that came surging up from nowhere. Last night, after she had rushed home believing she had lost James for good, or even an hour ago, walking miserably past the pub in the village, she had let herself take every bit of blame for everything that had gone wrong between them, and would have abjectly snatched at any chance to bring them together again. But now it seemed she was about to push them into another round of perhaps truly irrevocable recriminations, and there was nothing she could do to stop herself. 'It wasn't all my fault, James, and I won't take all the blame for it. I admit I was as silly as a rabbit, and immature and probably inconsiderate, but you must have known when you married me that, at nineteen, I had a lot of growing up to do.' Roz was feeling ominously calm and amazingly clearheaded. 'And I might have grown up faster if you'd treated me more as an equal—confided in me about your business worries or whatever was going on, and not treated me like an indulged child.'

'I didn't want to worry you,' James protested, feebly. 'And I thought I could handle things alone.'

'That's what I said—treated me like a child, protecting me from the not-so-nice realities and from the fact that you could be as worried and as vulnerable as the next man. You wanted me to think you could manage everything with one hand tied behind your back.' Roz gave an involuntary, bitter laugh. 'Well, you succeeded—I did think that, but how was I to know that underneath it all you were seething with resentment that you didn't have a woman to turn to when you needed her? I could have been that woman, James. I could have been there for you, but you never let me even try. And you weren't there for me, either.' To her horror, the prickling in her eyes turned into a cascade of hot tears down her cheeks. James seemed mesmerised by them—or by what was pouring out from behind her barrier of repressed hurt. His face was frozen into incredulous comprehension.

Roz made a quick dab at the tears with the back of her hand and struggled on. 'I didn't know what was happening to us; everything was changing and I didn't know why. I was scared you didn't want me any more, that you'd found someone else and were deliberately edging me out of your life until you were ready to leave me altogether. And so I had to find something else, too. And, when I did, I left—first. To spite you. And to prove I was capable of living my own life and that I didn't need you. But I do, damn it. Oh, hell!' The tears were streaming again; she couldn't see for them. 'I'm sorry. I'm not crying. This is stupid.' She rushed past him and started to run blindly along the path beyond the terrace.

James caught her before she had taken half a dozen steps. his arms closed around her, pulling her body around against his own and holding her, and Roz subsided into the mindless luxury of a good howl, the side of her face scratching against the knobbly pattern of James's sweater.

'There never was anyone else then, and there isn't anyone else now. It's always been you, Rosalind.' She felt his lips in her hair, his arms gathering her closer and more tightly. 'I'm sorry I ever made you think otherwise. I never meant to, darling, please believe me.'

Her heart believed him and that was a start; her mind would catch up soon, perhaps, but for the moment there were questions she wanted answered; assurances she needed to hear. Roz pulled her face away from James's chest and, fumbling a hanky out of the pocket, wiped her eyes, blew her nose and felt a whole lot better. She was past caring how she looked.

'If that's true, then why did you tell your solicitor to start divorce proceedings?' she demanded, the belligerence betraying how very insecure she could still feel, even with James's arms locked around her waist.

James smiled wincingly. 'To call your bluff, I suppose. And if it had backfired on me and I'd lost you...' He shrugged. 'Even that would have been more bearable than the tearing uncertainty I'd been living through all year, not to speak of the utter hell since you came back from Zangyria, when one minute I was insane with hope that we stood a chance of sorting ourselves out if only we'd talk, the next...' The shrug was angry this time. '...bashing my head against a brick wall because it seemed the only things that mattered to you were your independence and your career.'

Dangerous, dangerous ground. Leave it; don't rise to this bait and risk everything now, Roz begged herself. In vain. 'I might have acquired my career by default, but it's as important to me now as yours to you, James.' She kept her voice carefully even and unemotional, and saw from the tightening of James's face that he, too, was aware they had just hit a stretch of very thin ice.

'I don't think you really mean that,' he said quietly, and the unamused laugh that followed caught Roz by surprise, checking her reaction by at least four seconds.

'Oh, don't I just?' she retorted indignantly, and breaking out of the circle of his arms she started marching furiously along the path.

James fell into stride beside her. 'There's no need to bite my head off. All I meant was that you're making a mistake using my so-called career as a yardstick, and that I hope yours is a darned sight more important to you than mine is to me right now.'

Roz made a long groaning sound, and stopped in her tracks, stricken with shame. 'Oh, James, I'm sorry. I didn't think...I haven't asked...What's happening? You're not—you're not out on your ear, are you?' She couldn't get the breathless questions out quickly enough.

'Out on my ear?' The term made James chuckle. 'That sounds suspiciously like Ms Barett's colourful turn of phrase. The answer is, no, I'm not and yes, I am, and, if that smacks of the equivocation I've been accusing you of, it's only because it's true. McGinley has tactfully offered me the managing directorship, and the rules of the game are that I thank him and say I'll think about it, and then—tactfully, of course—refuse. They don't like old brooms hanging about, getting in the way of the new ones,' James explained, drily, but did not seem overly upset.

Roz found that baffling. 'But what will you do? What do you want to do?'

'What I've always wanted to do. What I was planning to do when Dad died and left me saddled with Allied Press—buy into some small quality weekly and take over the editorship. It would be a different sort of life, Rosalind, I promise,' James assured her earnestly, perhaps thinking her silence was doubt, whereas Roz was needing it to digest the information that James had been trapped for years in a position he couldn't wait to get out of. 'There'd be less hassles; I'd have more time at home; we could...'

'We could...what?' Roz prompted encouragingly; it had sounded more like the start of a hope than another promise.

They were walking again, heading towards the ornamental lake, but walking mainly for the sake of walking, not to get anywhere, because it seemed to make them more comfortable. 'We could what, James?' Roz repeated when James didn't answer.

James took her hand and slipped it through his arm. 'Do the things we planned. Live the sort of life we talked about.'

Roz understood immediately. 'Children, lots of them. Dogs...cats—the whole menagerie.' She quoted James's own words back at him on a sudden wave of joy at the second chance fate was dealing out to them.

James turned to her anxiously. 'And you could still have your career,' he pointed out urgently, as if she had momentarily overlooked it.

'Ah, yes, my "damned-fool hobby",' Roz quoted him again, teasingly.

'Oh, God, must you?' James groaned, mock serious but not so mock about the eyes. They looked pained. 'Darling, I never meant to be so obnoxious about your photography, but I was as scared as you were about what was happening to us, and I latched on to that as the most convenient thing to blame—mindless, knee-jerk reaction. I would never stand in the way of your career, Rosalind. I'm proud of what you've achieved, and I want you to continue. You know that, don't you?'

'I know that,' said Roz, her priorities well worked out in her mind. Yes, she would have her career, but it would be a part of her life from now on, and not its centre. Local jobs; Greece was out. She would tell James that later, tomorrow perhaps, or the day after. They had their whole lives to talk, have arguments, reach compromises. Now there were other things on her mind. James's too, it seemed; he stopped them short of the lake and took her in his arms.

'I love you. What do you say we go home now?' James asked softly after their kiss, his eyes telling her in warm, graphic detail what to expect when they got there.

Roz blushed, and said it sounded like a wonderful idea.

Harlequin American Romance

Romances that go one step farther...
American Romance

Realistic stories involving people you can relate to and care about.

Compelling relationships between the mature men and women of today's world.

Romances that capture the core of genuine emotions between a man and a woman.

Join us each month for four new titles wherever paperback books are sold.
Enter the world of American Romance.

Amro-1

ATTRACTIVE, SPACE SAVING BOOK RACK

Display your most prized novels on this handsome and sturdy book rack. The hand-rubbed walnut finish will blend into your library decor with quiet elegance, providing a practical organizer for your favorite hard-or soft-covered books.

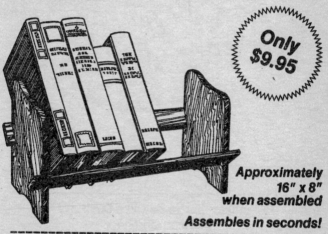

Only $9.95

Approximately 16" x 8" when assembled

Assembles in seconds!

To order, rush your name, address and zip code, along with a check or money order for $10.70* ($9.95 plus 75¢ postage and handling) payable to *Harlequin Reader Service*:

Harlequin Reader Service
Book Rack Offer
901 Fuhrmann Blvd.
P.O. Box 1396
Buffalo, NY 14269-1396

Offer not available in Canada.

BKR-1A

*New York and Iowa residents add appropriate sales tax.